Rebecca —
I wish you the best.
Thanks for playing and
for your time and
for your support.

EARPLUGS

Bram Riddlebarger

Livingston Press

The University of West Alabama

isbn 13: 978-1-60489-103-4, library binding
isbn 13: 978-1-60489-104-1, trade paper
Library of Congress Control Number 2012944361
Printed on acid-free paper.
Galleys printed in the United States of America by
Publishers Graphics

Hardcover binding by: Heckman Bindery
Typesetting and page layout: Joe Taylor
Proofreading: Morgan Jowers, Ginger Rutherford, Ashley Vaughn

Cover: Jana Vukovic

Acknowledgements:
Sarah, Mieke, Raney, Ever, Halle, Marilou, Jerry Gabriel, David Childers,
Joe Taylor, Patrick Somerville, CJ, Joan Connor, Redtails, Brian & Ben

"A Sixty-Two Cent Meal" appeared in *17 ½ Magazine* (Summer 2008).
"The Anatomy of a Band-Aid" appeared in altered form in *Aquabear Reader*
(Winter 2009).
"Ocean of Confusion" is a song title by the Screaming Trees.
"Same old blues" and "days full of rain" are from the song "Flyin' Shoes" by
Townes Van Zant.
The beginning of the chapter "Nature's Course" was inspired by Ghostwriter's
song "Maverick."

first edition

6 5 4 3 3 2 1

EARPLUGS

For Sarah

EARPLUGS

I lived in a small town, so went to buy earplugs. First to the north side and our dying strip mall, littered with the refuse of ancient names and outdated lives. Hmmm, Sporting Goods and Hardware, aisles ten and eleven.

"The trees are fruitless and out of season," said the clerk. "But I could sell you some wonderful apples."

"No thanks, I really just wanted earplugs."

"Well, OK, but my apples are really delicious!"

I saw that this man knew his fruit, but what this town needed, I told him, were earplugs.

I walked to the Hardware Store. The smell of our Hardware Store was renowned in the state. A sign hung over the door that said:

STOP IN FOR THE SMELL!

and many did. Despite our forests and our caves, our hardware store on Main Street was a beacon of smell and a must-do for any newcomer. I liked the hammer section the best, but many townspeople could often be seen lounging around the screwdriver aisle a little longer than necessary.

"Earplugs, huh?"

"Yeah, I need some earplugs."

"Nope, but I'll tell you what. Why don't you go try the seed section? The smell of those carrot seeds is just dandy!"

I glanced over. Ten or twelve locals and several tourists were gathered around the seed section in an aromatic orgasm.

"Looks tempting," I said. "But what I need are some earplugs."

"Earplugs, huh? No, I never much cared for the smell of earplugs," he sniffed.

I returned to the north side of town and into the Relics for All Purposes Store. One room full of shoes, guns, hardware, beach balls, and any number of such items except earplugs. The employees had not even heard of earplugs yet.

"In your ears, huh?"

She was amazed.

"What for?"

"Well, I'm not sure really. I just wanted some good earplugs," I said.

I beat a quick retreat past throwing knives and hickory axe handles.

Perhaps earplugs were just some crazed children's author's idea of a good joke.

"My, what big earplugs you have!"

I uneasily peeked into the Chainsaw and Heavy Equipment Store just outside town, only to be exposed by the deafening roar of a chainsaw motor rigged up to the door.

"Nice bell."

"Huh?"

"Nice bell."

"What?"

"NICE BELL!"

"Oh, yeah . . . you here for the weed-whacker special?"

I silently drifted aloft, now a turkey vulture soaring on a small-town thermal on a very loud day. From this vantage, the smell and the volume of town became faint and almost bearable. Across the Meandering River, I could see past our town limits and out into our lovely rolling foothills.

The view was a postcard.

Lisa was not around.

Tourists marched hither and yon, traipsing like schoolchildren in search of candy over forest and dale; but I could see no farther. I could not see Far Away. But I was not a turkey vulture, and my feet were again in search of earplugs.

"I should find some earplugs," I said.

Still thinking hardware equaled earplugs, I came to our town's Last and Certainly Most Forgotten Hardware and Lumber Store at the southern end of town. There was not much smell to this place. Despite its freeway-side locale, business and tourism had dropped to an all-time low. However, I chuckled to myself, this was likely the place to score earplugs.

My ears felt the silence and the comfort that must come with a brand new pair of earplugs. But they had no bargain on earplugs, because they had no earplugs. My ears and my disappointment lounged together in wicker boat chairs. They sipped piña coladas in the sunny world of our town's Salsa Vendor. They dipped tortilla chips into tongue-blistering salsa. Suddenly, the take-off of a very large airplane at a very close distance interrupted their tropical reverie. My ears and my disappointment then realized that they were sitting next to the largest airport runway in the world. My earlobes touched the tarmac. It was at least as loud as living in a small town.

"Earplugs, huh? I'll tell you what. Go up to my dad's barbershop on the north side. He's got some earplugs," the intercom crackled. "And please remember to remove your baggage from the aisles. Thank you."

One hour thirty-three minutes and seventeen seconds after leaving in search of earplugs, I began to hope.

But the barber was fresh out of earplugs.

"No, I'm fresh out of earplugs," he snipped. "Go over to my house and check my gun bag. . . . I might have some earplugs in my gun bag."

The gun bag held no earplugs. But the smell of his freshly oiled gun and the freshly picked apples his wife gave me were sure good. The barber told me that my theory on hardware equaling earplugs was where I was going wrong.

"Sporting goods . . . sporting goods is where the earplugs are at," he said, and off I went to the local Bait and Guns Shop outside town.

"Earplugs, huh? Nope, just sold all them to some guy come in here 'bout a week ago and bought up all my earplugs."

Perhaps everyone felt as I did. Perhaps Lisa was getting around. I began to question earplugs, but then I realized that I had rarely seen earplugs, let alone seen them in anyone else's ears. The Biddies did not wear them, but they were old.

"Why don'tcha go fishin' instead. I got some real pretty night crawlers—they don't talk much."

"I just need some earplugs," I faltered.

"Earplugs, huh? Well, hang on a second," said the Bait and Guns Shop owner.

I held on a second. Then another one. In fact, I held on 9,738 seconds.

But he never came back with earplugs.

"I don't think he's coming back with any earplugs," I said.

So I went to the library in the center of town to look for earplugs. The library had about three hundred pairs sitting on a shelf like mastodons on a clear day.

EARPLUGS

PICKLES AND MILKSHAKES

With a brand new set of earplugs in my ears, I stepped out onto the broken library sidewalk and enjoyed the new sensation of living in a small town and imagining something else.

"Hey! What are those goddamn blue things in your ears?" a small boy asked from a red tricycle.

I stared at his moving mouth like a silent picture and turned to go get a vanilla milkshake at the Rustic Drugstore.

The Rustic Drugstore was right in the middle of downtown. No one had noticed the drugstore for twelve years and forty-one days.

"Hey, did you see that?" a tourist or a middle-aged man might say to his companion, while passing by the Rustic Drugstore on a clear afternoon.

"No, I didn't see a thing," his companion would reply.

The companions would move on to Somewhere Else. That was how things went with the Rustic Drugstore. The drugstore was so well camouflaged in the center of downtown that soon no one would see it at all. As with many other businesses in town, the Rustic Drugstore would soon move out to the new I.C. Road like a drugstore spider willfully intent on snaring some easy tourist flies. The Rustic Drugstore was growing lean downtown. Sometimes baby needs a new pair of shoes. The owners were told that their new location on the I.C. Road would be a brightly colored sign in a forest of drab excitement, and that they had better get ready to make a lot more milkshakes, and of course to sell a lot more drugs.

They were also told about Competition and about when the time was right to Sell.

But while the drugstore hid downtown, playing peek-a-boo to no effect, I liked to drink the vanilla milkshakes sold at the luncheon counter of the Rustic Drugstore. Sometimes I would consider ordering a pop with a squirt of cherry- or vanilla-flavored syrup. An assortment of flavored syrups stood in a perfect line behind the luncheon counter like temptation soldiers, their silver pour-spouts held at full attention. But then I stuck with a vanilla milkshake. The milkshakes at the Rustic Drugstore were made with a heavy old milkshake maker and they tasted delicious. After the Rustic Drugstore moved out to the new highway, I heard that they no longer used that old metal milkshake maker. I also heard that the new milkshakes tasted like money-not-well-spent and that the Rustic Drugstore's flavored pop came only in aluminum cans.

As I drank my milkshakes, I would often pretend that I could not hear the voices that were not really there that sometimes told me to go and to buy earplugs and to save myself the trouble. Now that my earplugs were squashed firmly in place, I drifted silently over the black and white tile floor and into the rows of Forgotten Goods and Services. I stared at a plastic egg of pantyhose and headed for the luncheon counter at the back left-hand side of the store. I smelled fried onions and toasting hamburger buns like a childhood dream of arcade games and innocence.

"Could I have a vanilla milkshake?"

"PLEASE STOP YELLING!" the waitress yelled, as she reached for a bottle of ketchup.

I sat and drank my milkshake and did not hear the Only Other Customer in Town walk past me and sit down on a chrome stool. The Only Other Customer in Town liked to eat the BBQ sandwiches with pickles and lots of pepper that the rest of the town had forgotten about. No one else in town ever remembered to order the BBQ sandwich, which sat on the menu like an encrypted ancient language.

The Only Other Customer in Town ate his encrypted sandwich and enjoyed a hieroglyphic pickle that made little to no sense.

"I-IDLB-XXxiIEWL," he said. "P-VDEY-ZEE."

"Cucumber?"

I paid for my milkshake through a neon green forest of Technicolor bird feathers and low murmurous words that all started with C or Q and contained many X's and L's while natives wearing jaguar loincloths squatted on chrome luncheon stools eating BBQ beef sandwiches and toasted hamburger buns.

"QuLitalititLLLxL," parroted the waitress.

"Thank you. It was delicious."

"Yes. I do love pickles."

Far out in the dank daytime humid country air, the Salsa Vendor, enjoying his mid-day siesta, was startled awake as he slept in his salsa vendor shack. The time had come to pickle some peppers and to sing a sad ukulele song.

EARPLUGS

BEANS

Years ago, our town was plotted in the floodplain and along the dirty fields of the Meandering River. The Town Fathers and Mothers chose not to survey the west side. No one knew why. Plausible explanations tended to favor the lack of ambition. These days the west side was a jumbled deterioration of mobile homes and plastic yard ornaments, which sat like illicit leaves on the manicured, imaginary lawn of our Town Council's collective mind. Streets were not really streets at all and ran in no particular direction except Away. Once, the Only Other Customer in Town had failed to start a baked bean shop several doors down from my trailer. No one came.

"So I guess no one likes baked beans!" the Only Other Customer in Town had gassed, as he closed the Baked Bean Shop doors and headed off for a BBQ sandwich.

The wind merely blew around.

I thought of the idea of earplugs, and the idea of beans, and the idea of nuthatches, and not the idea of Lisa.

Things were like that here.

Before.

PORK RINDS

"Honey, I know you."

"You don't know what I feel."

"Yes. I do."

"You say you do, but you don't."

"I'm leaving," said Lisa.

And she left.

I went for a vanilla milkshake. I passed over the familiar black and white tile of the Rustic Drugstore and sat down on one of the chrome stools at the luncheon counter. The Only Other Customer in Town was eating a BBQ sandwich from a small paper plate. There were two hamburger pickle slices and many fine grains of ground black pepper on the white plate. As I sat at the counter, I thought of Lisa and the town as if I were a paper drinking straw slurping the last sugary drops from its third seven-ounce green glass bottle of 7-UP. I had not yet found earplugs; I had heard every word Lisa said. A snack-sized bag of pork rinds with a dipping bowl of chili sauce sat beside the green glass bottle in my mind. The pork rinds crunched loudly. The green bottle was smooth, except for a ridge around the textured white and red paint of the logo.

Running mental fingers over the bottle, beads of sweat dripped and fell down the glass like tears, or cum, or the sad rapid passage of time. The paper drinking straw hung limply then, flaccid against the mouth of the green glass bottle in my mind.

"I love pork rinds," said the Only Other Customer in Town.

I ate such a snack as a youth when I played at my grandfather's bar—how the paper drinking straw would pulp with time. Childhood games of "Red Light, Green Light" down the long, dim aisle of the wooden bar. The wood pitted and scarred. Its grain of smoke and time. While we played, my grandfather cleaned beer mugs and shot glasses and kept silent on the Sunday afternoons when the bar shut down for the day. Time stood still like ghost-children stuck forever on "Red Light."

Laughter and innocence echoed up through the ages and stopped now.

Through a hard plastic drinking straw, I sucked the last of my vanilla milkshake and thought again about earplugs, and about how I should probably go and get some.

That bar was long gone.

So was grandpa.

But the idea of earplugs was there.

Right then.

THE ANATOMY OF A BAND AID

She wore green sweatpants and a neon pink headband that afternoon like an Easter basket on an ominous day. The Easter basket was filled with empty calories that sparkled in shiny packages and inside were morsels of prescient, if fleeting, bliss. The morsels tasted good, and I thought that they would last longer.

This was the first time that I saw Lisa. Before earplugs. She ran jogging past my front window in green sweatpants, and her long blonde hair was pulled back in a knot. The pink headband wrapped around her head, but did not quite keep the long bangs away from her panting face. Nuthatches pecked and flew at my bird feeder. Then Lisa tripped. I ran outside like a blue-faced hero in an epic movie about good and bad and loyalty and devotion and things that hurt to help her.

As I ran I prayed, O, brave heart, fortify my undernourished social skills and give me the grace that this poor girl clearly may lack.

Sitting on the dirty road, Lisa hissed in pain. "*Ssffffff,*" she said, through wrinkled lips. She pulled up a green sweatpants leg to expose a beautiful, bleeding knee. The scrape was like blood pudding that had never found a casing. Instead, the scrape was now separating and oozing liquid from solid like a high school chemistry experiment in platelets and fibrin.

"I have some alcohol and dressing in my place," I said. "I'll get some if you like."

"No salad?"

"I mean some band-aids."

We went inside, and I band-aided her leg. As I placed a band-aid on the wound, I tenderly said all the words that I thought would make us last forever and ever. We kissed and made love, and then we made love again. Lisa went and picked up her things and moved in with her torn green sweatpants.

"I feel pretty good here," said Lisa.

"I could use some more salad," I said. "And then we could watch a movie or something."

We did not leave the house for several weeks. Stagnation set in like an infection. Band-aids were used and then, before long, instead of bandaging our wounds, we became the two separate white backing pieces that had once been happily attached in sticky band-aid Oneness. Time peeled us mindlessly Away from the Whole and threw us in the trash. A broken trinity of healing helplessness. Detritus on the relationship by-way. The need for new quests to fulfill our time.

My prospects were dim.

Her sweatpants were made for running, and they ran.

I was alone again and things were loud.

PAGES __ THROUGH __

After Lisa left and I had drunk too many milkshakes at the Rustic Drugstore, I came back home to sleep and to think about earplugs, but then I woke up with a terrible cold. The cold lasted so long that each day became a picture painted with acrylic-oil paint; this was a picture book cold, except longer. This cold exceeded all expectations in the publication of short picture books. This cold did not care about the attention spans of young children or about the average time that bored parents allotted to read picture books to their young ones before bedtime. No, this cold had other ideas. This cold felt more akin to a novella by a demented Eric Carle. This novella involved transformation and need and lots of dark, swirling colors and toilet paper for Kleenex. The cold was tired of reading *A Very Hungry Caterpillar* to ailing children every night and wanted to push the boundaries of reality and dream into a new frontier. The working title for this cold was *Infirmary, and Beyond (illustrated)*.

My Only Friend in Town tried to help me, but he just prolonged my condition.

"Buck up, man," said My Only Friend in Town. "Eat these."

I ate three chalky-dry mushrooms, and my life transformed and became more swirls of colors, and pages upon pages, and sickness upon sickness. I turned the pages of the demented Eric Carle sickness and analyzed the intricate brushwork with patience and perception. One week I turned to page one hundred-and-six. It was the foreshadowed sequel of page thirty-two. The brushstrokes were thick, and heavy, and still slightly wet.

Outside my trailer, town. The sound deafening. The smell repugnant. The weight overbearing.

Band-aids and salads had passed. Nice green leaves were not available for consumption. I had become stuck forever on a new concept for Swiss cheese, ice cream cones, salami, and sickness.

My Only Friend in Town stopped coming to see me.

"I don't want to catch that shit," said My Only Friend in Town.

Orange juice, and mushrooms, and chicken noodle soup dissolved Away, but the cold keep on, marching resolutely toward novel-hood and that Great Beyond.

I sat around lethargically listening to our town and the river simper and crash and roar and bellow through my thin trailer walls. I found myself returning to leaf through one particular chapter of the picture book cold. The pages of this section held blurry images that were drawn into the book a month or so into the sickness. I was a different person. Mad eyes and no earplugs. In my favorite image, spring had painted itself around each corner and danced with sunlight green grass and big sky blues. The brush strokes were light, dry, and gay. The cold was far along then, and the main scene was all bleary like cloudy 2AM moonlight.

Then in that moment of every unrelenting sickness, that cocoon of suspension, when the clouds of infirmary finally begin to part, I stared at those weeks of pictures and felt the world reconfigure into a rebirth. A renewal. Another idea. All time and space became focused on other possibilities. From the depths of dementia, I thought again about earplugs. Perhaps there was something else; no, not a beautiful butterfly, but earplugs.

Earplugs were the answer to town and to the problem of Lisa.

"You sick?" townspeople would ask, as I ventured out.

"Mm-hmm," I would sniffle.

"What's wrong with you?"

"It's loud."

"Loud?"

"Yes."

"Haven't seen you around for a few weeks."

"No."

"Maybe you should find the doc. The hospital's around here somewhere."

"Uh-huh."

Sniff.

"Do you smell that?"

"Uh-uh."

"Aww. Biddies."

I eventually felt better and went to buy earplugs.

PINEAPPLE SALSA AND PINTO BEANS

I walked out of the Rustic Drugstore and inserted a fresh set of earplugs into my ears. Birds chirped like mimes. Far up the street, I saw green sweatpants jogging Away: Lisa. I headed to the west side of town to look at the river. I would watch the river for several hours and then I would walk home to eat canned pinto beans with pineapple salsa. I bought the pineapple salsa at our local Farmer's Market. The Farmer's Market took place on Wednesday mornings down in the middle of town by the Civil War Veterans for Either Side Memorial. The memorial sat in the middle of our small downtown park, as indecisive as ever, and the salsa you could buy for a song because, well, it was pineapple salsa. Most people in town had not even heard of pineapples, much less tasted one mixed up with chili peppers, cumin, and pureed heirloom tomatoes.

"They won't like it," predicted My Only Friend in Town. "Foreign things are just too foreign. It's like, if it comes from Somewhere Else, it probably doesn't even exist at all."

For once, My Only Friend in Town was right.

"Pineapple, huh? That like the fruit inside a pine cone or

somethin'?" townspeople would ask the Salsa Vendor, upon seeing the new pineapple salsa.

"No," our ninety-three year old Salsa Vendor would reply. "The pineapple, cultivated throughout the Pacific, is a tropical, herbaceous perennial native to South America, whose fruit looks somewhat like a pine cone, except that it isn't as small and doesn't grow on coniferous appendages. It does, however, resemble that growth on your alligator-like feet, except there are sharp, spiky green leaves sticking out of the top. And it's very sweet."

Six years ago, the Salsa Vendor had decided it was high time to see the world. He had lived his whole life within the confines of our county like a hermit crab with a county shell. The shell fit fine for eighty-seven years, but then it seemed a bit snug about his shoulders.

On the Salsa Vendor's maiden mosey beyond our county line, he paid a visit to our state capital. The state capital lay fifty-two miles north of our town, a vision of sled dogs and cold weather bedding down for a six-month night of ineffective public governance and terrible food.

While touring the capital city, the Salsa Vendor took photographs, picked up tomatoes, and vowed to make a better salsa than he had eaten for lunch that day at an outrageously expensive downtown restaurant named Olé. Olé served fusion fare, and it was not good.

"More like con-fusion," said the Salsa Vendor. "I can do better than that."

The expensive meal cost the equivalent of twenty-eight and a half jars of salsa.

The Salsa Vendor said, "And I will."

The following week he booked passage on a seagoing freightliner and headed for places not found on the Only Map Around.

"I wonder where the Salsa Vendor's at?" townspeople wondered, as they drank their morning coffee and noticed the empty place beside the park where the Salsa Vendor set up his little salsa vending stand.

"He must have gone Somewhere Else," indicted the town prosecutor, as he climbed the sandstone steps of the Courthouse.

"I can't imagine where he would have gone off to," said a passing Biddy. "At his age."

The Salsa Vendor was like a missing piece in the jigsaw puzzle of our town.

"I hope he comes back soon," said the clerk of courts. "I'm almost out of piccalilli."

The Salsa Vendor did return. He arrived back in town from his virgin voyage as if he were Christopher Columbus bearing strange and exotic foodstuffs that would soon become salsa. He wore an alpaca suit. He wore a sailor tattoo. He took up the culinary *nom de guerre* of Veteran Master Salsa Vendor and then sold a jar of chutney to the clerk of courts. He strummed a ukulele. He sang songs that no one could understand.

Songs of pineapple gibberish.

"Huh. Pineapple. And you eat it with what?"

"I told you," said My Only Friend in Town.

I bought the whole batch for two dollars. I ate pineapple-flavored pinto beans for months. I became a South Seas ranch hand looking at the stars around a dim campfire every night while thinking of hula skirts and exotic women that were not Lisa, but often had Lisa's face.

Next to the Old Iron Trestle, a neon pink headband lay quietly on a rock. I stayed by the river for three hours and thought of things that see and do not move, and then I left to go for my beans.

"I should go for my beans," I thought. I tried not to think of hula skirts or Lisa.

"I'm pretty hungry," I said.

The river was thirsty, too.

MY ONLY FRIEND IN TOWN

After dinner, I left and crossed the dirt to see My Only Friend in Town. My Only Friend in Town lived in a small red shack with white trim one hundred and eighteen feet from my trailer on the west side of town. A few years before, My Only Friend in Town had played music in a band. The band toured around the country for a short time, performing in dive bars and hip bars and small watering holes that all smelled the same. The band had tried hard to succeed, playing as if they were a new food product in the world-wide scheme of food products, though really they were just peanut butter and jelly. The peanut butter was spread on a piece of white bread, and the jelly was too, and together they formed a peanut butter and jelly sandwich. The name of the band should have been Peanut Butter and Jelly Sandwich, but it was not. The band's memory and their brief time on the road followed My Only Friend in Town like the lingering smell of cigarette smoke in his black cotton sweat jacket, which had been worn on too many hot afternoons. The leftover smell was musky and vaguely unpleasant and left My Only Friend in Town habitually advising our townspeople on the ways and the means of the world. My Only Friend in Town also drank a lot of

EARPLUGS

beer and was usually thinking that he could have been better.

"So, how was the river?" yelled My Only Friend in Town.

"Meandering like a graduating high school class in search of its destiny."

"I like the way that sounds," sang My Only Friend in Town. "Except this one time I was in Des Moines, they didn't treat me so well, and I don't want to go back to Iowa."

"I hear it's flat there," I clapped. I held a beer bottle in one uninterested hand. I had heard this song one thousand times before. He was My Only Friend in Town.

We played video games for hours. The graphics and stilted, if muffled, dialogue of the video game drove the sound and the smells of town completely from my mind. Lisa ceased to exist. The Biddies and the Service Industry dissolved Away. My Only Friend in Town and I transformed into a teenaged Peking Man and a pair of canvas hi-top sneakers sitting together on a couch. Peking Man and the sneakers were playing video games at Peking Man's parents' house, eating powdered-cheese-covered corn chips, drinking pop, and having a really good time. Upstairs, their babysitter, Innocence, sat at a table reading an oceanic magazine, and the fat kid from down the street, Worldly Troubles, was still knocking at the front door, waiting to be let in. That was how it had gone for years. But things change. Now My Only Friend in Town and I drank beer and rolled joints of Boredom Relief and tried not to think too much about the town and about the troubles, which had long since ransacked the place anyway.

Blip. Blip.

"Yeah!"

I lost every game.

Three wins in, My Only Friend in Town stopped trying to yell victory chants through my earplugs and began to scream only at the television monitor, which sounded mostly like:

"Mmuff-Muff-Ffhum-foodle"

And, "Buff-moof-ARRRRRR."

I soon left and did not hear the door hit my ass on the way out.

I walked over to the Old Iron Trestle and again watched the river. The water looked sleek and cold and mounds of brown silt rose up in spots like the idea of Huck Finn and Jim and the great American tale. The clouds changed into ghosts, and the sky began to think about getting dark. The pink headband still lay on the rock. I thought about taking out my earplugs, but then I went home to sleep and to dream of quieter things.

THE ROUND HOUSE

There was a peculiar house to the northwest of our town. This peculiar house lay just past the town limits as if it were a Victorian hemline on the outskirts of our town. The house was a round house, so people in town called it the Round House. The Round House sat in a little glade of our tourist-friendly trees like a giant white puffball mushroom with windows. No one remembered who built the Round House. It was long ago, and things were less certain then. Perhaps it was built to resemble the moon or to resemble Another Place. Or maybe it was built to make up for a life that one had not lived before. Either way, the Round House stood forlorn, condemned, and quiet, like an empty canister of fuel on a failed mission to Somewhere Else.

I went to the Round House to escape our town, as a pilgrim might in the flood of ecstasy and light and hand-waving, gyroscopic delirium. There was that smell. That growing smell. Like an ancient god, induced by old age and a need to mask the ripe, had been passing a long and sustained series of stinkers all over our town. Except the god in this case was the Biddy Brigade, and the scent was a particular scent. For most of the hand-waving, gyroscopic delirium those days was done exclusively in front of one's nose, a useless and futile attempt to ward off the gaseous smell of the Biddies and their odious perfume: Eau de Auld.

"They're messin' up the seed section," complained the Hardware Store manager. "How're we gonna do business without our smell?"

"Time," the Service Industry prophesied, "will tell."

In the Round House, I sat on a broken stone like a prism of what could have been and watched dust motes travel in the sunshine. The sunshine coursed through the cracked window panes and crisscrossed the round, dirty floor at unusual angles. I could not hear our town, which sometimes resembled the dust motes before we settled into our ways.

The Biddies and their smell were Far Away.

The town's complaints were echoes of time.

A day after leaving slain digital comrades scattered like New Age cannon fodder across a milieu of red, green, and blue pixels at My Only Friend in Town's place, I sat in the Round House and examined a dragonfly that had flown over from the river for a visit. This dragonfly did not seem ordinary. The colors on the insect changed and turned like a solar kaleidoscope.

I ate a Boston Baked Bean, and the bug flew off.

I sat in the Round House for two and a half hours and listened for sounds from the river. I wondered about that pink headband on the rock and the illusion of colors. Colors expanding and refracting. Little white lies of separation and betrayal. A rainbow of heartache and mystery and change.

"We always see things too late," I said.

I stood up from the broken stone, and I left.

BOSTON BAKED BEANS AND THE LOOMING SMELL OF THE BIDDY INQUISITION

I walked around our small-town downtown, gazing in at the hopeless window display cases: widow-schlepping. A motley assortment of doomed local start-up businesses rotated in and out of the low rent buildings. There were always one or two cheerleading, dance, or martial arts instructors willing to give it one more try, bilk a few more bucks. There was nothing else to do anyway. Their gold-chromed trophies stood in their soap-scrawled windows like advertisements, champions of nothing in a land of Nowhere.

The majority of our once stately downtown buildings stood bereft and hollow. Business was a dream thought up by the Meandering River and carried Far Away. Through these buildings' grimy storefront windows, receipts, rosters, playbills, Masonic regalia, and broken-keyed pianos, could just be seen scattered here and there on the hard wooden floors, like drowned sailors in a sea of dust. The owners prayed daily for fire.

"I'm thinking of starting up a used clothing store," planned the Only Other Customer in Town. "The poor can always sell clothes again to the poorer. I think it'll work. I'll name it Hand-Me-Down-Me-Downs."

A few long term businesses remained. Like old trees, these survivors stoically weathered the changing times. They had lost a few branches. They had been kicked by small children. Girdling had occurred via weed-whacker. But these stores had missed the fickle consumer axe. The majority sold or displayed carbon in various states of temperament. My favorite of the old-timers was a three-way tie between the Hardware Store, Bejeweled Trinkets, and Leo's, which perhaps was not a tie at all, but Leo's was my sugar dealer daddy. Leo's sold Boston Baked Beans in small cardboard boxes for ten cents a box. The boxes smelled and tasted remarkably like the stale brown candies contained within them.

"I prefer Zero bars myself," chortled the Only Other Customer in Town, standing outside the future Sandstone Cliffs with Pretty Hills and Classy Food Restaurant. "Back when I could get one, I liked to eat a Zero bar after a delicious BBQ sandwich on a toasted hamburger bun at the Rustic Drugstore. The white nougat was a nice complement to a good BBQ beef sandwich with pickles and lots of pepper. Of course, I also prefer baked beans. The real ones. Like we have here in Baked Bean City."

"BBQ sandwich at the Rustic Drugstore?" asked a townsperson.

Leo's occupied a once coveted position on the corner of Main

Street and Mulberry Street, next door to the Crumbling Theater. During its heyday, the Crumbling Theater had been a beacon of entertainment on any weekend—matinee or feature. But the Crumbling Theater lay abandoned. Inside its walls, the ghost of buttered popcorn floated over worn red velvet seats. The off-white movie screen hid in shadows and dust. Petrified gum layered its floor. Long dead exit signs occasionally screamed "Fire! Fire!" for their own amusement. The projector spun a timeless movie: Stillness.

The Only Cineplex Around was now very Far Away.

A classic five and dime, Leo's had a two-door system. A customer walked in the right hand entrance and picked up a loaf of bread, a can of pop, a girlie magazine, a package of cigarettes, or Boston Baked Beans, and then did an inverse U to the cash register and left hand exit and got the hell out. It was a good system and did not require explanation. For longer perusal, the Hardware Store across the street offered all the goods in town, and everyone knew it. I bought five boxes of Boston Baked Beans and ate them hurriedly. Then I thought about our town, and about Lisa, and about how things were quieter now.

Downtown, nothing moved.

I walked north on Main Street and looked back twice for signs of the Biddy Inquisition. Its specter loomed like sauerkraut wafting all over our town.

SATURDAY MORNING TELEVISION

Sometimes the town was my enemy. It just seemed pregnant with kids that would grow up like memories to resent me with my earplugs and with my comforting sense of lower volumes.

"I HATE YOU," a ghost-child screams angrily into my muffled ears.

"Perhaps we can work this out."

"I'LL NEVER LISTEN TO YOU," the wispy children's sheet yells, like a cartoon on Saturday morning television.

"But the mountains are very far from here and yodeling isn't necessary," I reasoned back.

But it made little difference which scenario I devised in my plugged-up head. Our town could not be trusted when it came to ghost children, and they certainly would not listen anyway.

"I'm leaving," I said.

And I walked away to Somewhere Else, which does not exist at all.

ON THE MARCH

It was the daytime that I did not like, with all that was there and meaningful and important like it had eyes that could see. Not like the nighttime, when it was dark and I could see the stars. Everything was grounded then, and I knew why I was there. The ground below my feet. The weight of my body on the earth. The vast distance to Now. I believed in this like a good song that played on my stereo. It was the answer to the question in my mind of goosebumps and transcendence; there was a relationship between here and there and Somewhere Else, though really I knew that I was still just here.

I looked at the stars and pondered these thoughts as I walked over to My Only Friend in Town's place. I needed social contact. This was a week after I had visited the trestle and seen the vision of American literary greatness, which turned out to be so much accumulated silt wasted down from too much erosion and too much fertilizer washing away into the rivers and thus onward into the dying seas. I dropped in to see if My Only Friend in Town would give me some whiskey before I had to leave.

"You wanna shot? Beer? Both?"

"Sure. Not a shot. But I'll have some."

"OK."

"Neat. No ice."

"OK. OK."

In the kitchen I could hear the sound of ice not leaving the plastic ice tray willingly. "I'm having some trouble with the ice. . . ." *BAM! BAM!*

"No, no. No ice. I don't need any ice," I yelled.

"You don't want ice?"

"No. Just straight is fine."

"You sure? You don't want ice?"

"What?"

"YOU SURE? YOU DON'T WANT ANY ICE?"

"No. No, that's fine."

"YOU SURE?"

"No, that's fine."

"OK."

We drank bourbon and socialized and traded important truths like wampum beads and harmony, and then we went our separate ways.

"See you," said My Only Friend in Town.

He turned back to his video games and his long thoughts of past nights on small-town stages across America, and he thought that perhaps he could have done better.

"I could have done better," said My Only Friend in Town.

He cracked open another beer. The television screen blinked.

I headed to the lonely side of town. Glancing up at the stars, I stumbled on a brick that protruded from an unmaintained brick sidewalk. That was when I smelled it again: Eau de Auld.

"Aww," I said.

Trouble was afoot.

The Biddy Brigade was on the march.

THE BIDDY BRIGADE

The Biddy Brigade was comprised of old women wearing awful perfume: Eau de Auld.

Sniff.

"Hmm, you smell something?" a townsperson would say.

Sni—.

"Aww. Biddies."

Though they predominately lived in enclaves in the rolling hills outside town, Biddies were everywhere. You would run into them at the Grocery Store, at church, at our town's Fourth of July Jamboree and Fireworks Display, at community sports league games, at bake sales, of course at our town's high school football games, and on the sidewalks wandering around looking for someone, anyone, to talk to. But it was not until the time of the Service Industry's first maniacal grab for Power in the Name of Tourism that the Biddy Brigade's efforts had taken a new turn. Biddies drenched in Eau de Auld began to appear around town like road-killed skunks in spring. The agent became so powerful that it kept legions of townspeople at bay in their homes and dispelled the notion of a police force in our quaint tourist-friendly community.

Such was the Biddies' moral standing in line with the good of society.

"Those Biddies just smell bad. They're good, honest, and righteous citizens. Decent folks. This town doesn't need us anymore. Those Biddies can handle it," said the Last Police Chief in Town, on his way out the fraternal door.

The downside of town Biddy patrols, besides the smell, was that tourism suffered terribly. This was most noticeable in the seed section at the Hardware Store.

"Carrot seeds? It smells like death to me," said a disgruntled tourist, who had driven from five hours Away.

The editor of our town paper, the *Local Daily*, briefly considered changing the local forecast to Smelly, but then thought better of it and just printed the symbol for Old Man Winter.

The Salsa Vendor, out in his Salsa Vendor shack, was hit by a gust of Eau de Auld and suddenly inspired to create three new salsas.

"Fenugreek Curry!" exclaimed the Salsa Vendor. "Kimchi Habanero! Creamed Corn Queso-Teleggio!"

The gagging, wheezing, and rank atmospheric conditions caused by the ubiquitous smell of Eau de Auld took their toll. Our mayor, the Service Industry, was not pleased. As the Brigade baked apple pies and sweet potatoes in their county enclaves, members of Town Council and the entire staff of one at the mayor's office began to conspire. Lost tourist revenue was breaking the Service Industry's manipulative heart; incorporation was on our Council's mind.

But the Biddies had been around.

A long time.

Through the backchannels of the Long Vines of Endless Gossip, the Biddies caught wind of Council's planned municipal takeover and immediately launched a series of Walk-A-Thons through town that had everyone back inside. Someone on Council petitioned, unsuccessfully, to have Main Street renamed the Sea of Gray.

Commerce was suffering.

"This town stinks," said a fleeing tourist. "I'm outta here."

The war was on.

Like young children with parentally pre-defined neighborhood boundaries, My Only Friend in Town and I were relatively safe if we stayed close to our homes; the west side of town was not commercially zoned. This made the west side largely exempt from the ever-increasing Biddy patrols. There was a decided lack of elderly cares on the west side. In fact, there was a decided lack of the most basic civic amenities. Paved roads, handicapped parking spaces, sidewalks, VFW's, stop signs, pharmaceutical dispensaries—these things did not exist on the west side, and their absence severely hampered the Biddies' attempts for total control of our town.

Many people were confused when entering the west side.

Tourists that strayed there left quickly. They did not turn around in a mud-caked driveway. They sped around the block. The west side was entombed from Away. If services had existed on the west side, perhaps the Biddies would have braved crossing the Mighty Bridge, coaxed from their haven-like hills and the other well-stocked, planned, and funded sectors of town. Perhaps tourist dollars would have created jobs.

But no.

The west side was across the river and poor. Except for our mayor, the Service Industry, and her friend, Fast Food, no one much cared for the west side and its glut of uninsured workers.

But, O, the rusted, old Mighty Bridge.

The Mighty Bridge stood like a grizzled soldier-at-arms at the western gateway of our town. For decades, the bridge had ferried us safely from one muddy bank to the next. The bridge had tamed the Meandering River and only generously allowed the water to pass below its faded green trusses. The Mighty Bridge, before being torn down by the Service Industry, was a totem of what made the world pass in our town, and against its veiled beating pulse, rusted as it was, both Town Council and the Biddies alike cowered like dope fiends in the hoosegow.

For the Mighty Bridge did not care about perfume, or Tourism. It was constructed in the old times, when crossing the bridge to the Old Mill was the extent of our local agrarian economy. The fields grew the corn, the river turned the millstone, and our town survived. Canal boats and sturdy flat boats floated barrels of meal down the bottleneck Meandering River, and the farmers went home to grow more corn.

"Time to grow more corn," the farmers would say.

The bridge spanned the decades of hard times, resource depletion, and local pride. Now, the bridge was old. The Mill had moved to the south side of town, mechanized first by the Long Gone Railroad, then by the freeway, and now kept busy grinding imported Canadian wheat.

The Service Industry, at her desk in the stifling bureaucratic air of our ancient Mayoral Office, patiently plotted the Mighty Bridge's demise.

"I can't wait to have this place renovated," dreamed the Service Industry, as beads of sweat swelled beneath her Revlon. "And that bridge. We need a new bridge—sleek—flat—concrete—adorned with welcoming flowers. That's what we need. Tourist-friendly and impartial."

The Mighty Bridge swayed in the air over the Meandering River and said, "Fuck that."

The march of Modern Business encroached down the Inbound Commerce (I.C.) Road toward the Mighty Bridge and our town. An advance cavalcade of commerce charged ahead like a Trojan horse full of cheap, plastic toys.

Roads littered with trash.

Polluted creeks polluted again.

Fast Food floated under the Mighty Bridge in a slick new canoe.

The Biddies held control of town. Entrance up the Missed Tourist Dollar (M.T.D.) Road—named in a rallying fit of rage by a galvanized town populace to band together for god's sake to get what we got while the got's for the getting, a move spearheaded by a young and ambitious Service Industry—gave the Brigade access to all sectors of town except the west side. Eau de Auld coalesced. The Endless Chatter of Monotony survived. The Biddies spread their down-home word and upwind scent like childhood déjà vu complacency via nasal ingestion.

But things change. The Service Industry was also on the march.

And Commerce had her back.

THE ENDLESS CHATTER
OF MONOTONY

My earplugs had dampened the Endless Chatter of Monotony, the Biddy Brigade's other, perhaps equally powerful, tool. With that force minimized, little explanation of the Chatter's lasting devices will be dealt with at length. Intense boredom would ensue. Perhaps the reader would prefer to stroll down to his or her local dentist's office for a botched root canal, or maybe dream of a purgatorial eternity punctuated only by your local preacher's most dreary sermon — something on the order of Acts 17:16-34. Or maybe sit in traffic. Forever. With no electronic entertainment devices, only crushing motors, and honking horns, and that uncomfortable feeling that you really have to pee, right now, but know that you must wait at least another two hours and countless miles of workaday stasis.

"That's what it was always like on tour," said My Only Friend in Town.

Then again one could just live in a small town as I did — the silence, the weight, the monotony, the boredom. Alas, the Chatter calls. It wants to be heard. It has to be heard. The Endless Chatter of Monotony unfurls:

Several weeks after achieving earplugs, I went for a cream-filled doughnut at the Donut Shoppe and Bakery downtown. Without nasal premonition or provocation, I was Biddy-whacked on Main Street. The Biddy had come up downwind on a routine patrol, and I missed her malodorous scent like an unlucky buck shot down from a hunter's blind.

Donuts provided the Biddy's cover. In the early morning hours on Main Street, the delicious smell of rising yeast and baking donuts seeped from the Donut Shoppe's aging storefront windows and vents. The smell swirled in a frosty, trans-fat-glaze-inducing hallucination.

"Come and eat," beckoned the donuts.

The Hardware Store had not yet opened its seed section doors. Leo's was still locked up tight. The Only Other Customer in Town had not yet arrived. Blame the donut. Only the smell of freshly baked donuts or freshly baked apple pies could briefly hold Eau de Auld at bay.

I was donut-blind.

I was also thinking about Lisa, and about torn green sweatpants, and was clearly distracted.

As the Biddy approached, the good bakery smell fell away and was replaced by the laboratory-coat smell of cheap, fake floral bouquets in a summer funeral home. I realized that Eau de Auld was close. I thought briefly of inventing noseplugs, as the

Wright Brothers might have done if they had had big dreams on a rotten day. Perhaps noseplugs could have taken me Somewhere Else, transported me to Another Place, but the Endless Chatter of Monotony had already set in.

"I haven't seen you in church for a while, young man," a seventy-four year old, sure-as-the-stench-wreaking-from-her-aged-skin Biddy whirred at me. I gagged and chewed the last sugary bean from a now empty package of ten-cent Boston Baked Beans. I ceased to think about sex or about cream-filled donuts.

Instead, squirming, I tried to think about earplugs like high-density impact barriers of sound-proof blue board.

"We miss seein' you there," said the wretched Biddy.

"Well," I squirmed.

I imagined Red Rider BB guns, and family Christmases, and suffocating atmospheres, unable to fully quash the shrill sound of the Biddy's voice at two paces.

The Biddy chattered and blathered and pinched my metaphorical cheeks.

"My heavens!"

And the Chatter raged on.

"I can't believe how much you've grown. Etc."

I pushed against my blue earplugs, squashing decibels like ants, but stood strangely transfixed. I became a small child gazing for the first time upon a costumed Santa Claus, unable to break free from the Biddy's endless voice as it droned on and on and on and on.

I had also stepped in a big glob of bubblegum on the sidewalk. The bubblegum stuck to the bottom of my canvas sneaker and held me in place as if I were gravity and the gum were a sticky and malevolent black hole.

"OK. Well, I hope to see you again soon. So how's your uncle doing? I haven't seen him in years. Etc."

"Squirm."

"My, you've grown so much. Now who is your father again? I get all those boys mixed up. So the ball team is doing well? I don't get out so much anymore, but I try to listen on the radio."

"I don't play on the team." Squirm.

"You don't? I thought you did. Well. OK."

"You know, I can't really hear you so well, Mrs. Biddy," I finally managed to say. I gagged on the overripe fumes of Eau de Auld. The smell encased my head in a musky fog. The fog smelled like rotting wheat inside a grain storage bin. The smell was terrific. It was the third worst smell that I had ever smelled.

"Oh well, I'm pretty old," said the unrelenting Biddy. "I don't make it out so much anymore." Ramble. Ramble. "So what's your mother up to these days? . . . Etc?"

After ninety-three more minutes like statues, my forced smile cracked apart like a cheap toy in a cereal box, and I turned and retreated to the Winding Trails above our town. The Winding

Trails above town held mystic but useless powers. There was no better place to pretend that you were alone. The cemetery below the Winding Trails added weight to the matter like childhood memories of Easter eggs and rolling rocks and heavy tombstones with dirt. Far across the valley, beyond the Meandering River and outside town, the Lone Tree stood like a crucifixion on a bald, well-kempt hill. I had never been to the Lone Tree. It never seemed to grow. It never seemed to die. It had grown there throughout my life, perhaps as some untenable testament to the solitary and unapproachable. An unknowable. A dark shape fending off the wolves of some -ism that you did not like much but that looked peculiarly like common buckthorn, or multiflora rose, or some other field-munching scrub wood of our region that first tended to encroach upon any cleared field in our pretty, tourist-friendly hills.

Invasive species.

I walked these paths and listened to the woods.

I took my earplugs out. O, the Winding Trails. The sound was alive and held meaning. I heard the freeway on the other side of the valley like decay and rebirth, commerce and longing. A constant moving sound against the still leaves that surrounded the trails and the chattering squirrels. I moved farther into the forest and recalled memories from my youth of blown bicycle tires and baseball cards. I thought of cheap, brittle, cornstarch-covered bubble gum and Bazooka Joe and haircuts. I thought about the dog that I used to keep as a boy. I thought of tractors and dirt and mother's milk and the railroad tracks that My Only Friend in Town and I had once walked as if we were bearded ascetics in search of Truth—though we found only barking dogs. I thought of death and Mark Twain and where the twain shall meet; old songs and lullabies flowed through my brain like skiffs on a memory river. I thought of recess and of dodge ball and of the great schism between the social classes of our town: the poor, the poorer, a big pink rubber ball smacking into the poorest. I thought of dirt floors and then Lisa. I thought about benediction and about how hungry I was now.

With a peace like fasting flowing through my bones, I headed back to the library for more earplugs.

O, the hard red passage of time.

I had emptied my last box.

WATER AND ROW SEVENTEEN

Back on the thin brown carpet of the Walls of Knowledge Library, a malaise hung in the air like the leftover smell of Boston Baked Beans in an empty cardboard package. The feeling drifted about the circulation desk, and the magazine racks, and the unfilled book return bin, and back through me. I ducked down for a warm sip of water from the library's mineral-encrusted drinking fountain. Like a proboscis, my tongue darted in and out for a taste — a sinister slurp, a foul wetting of the whistle; the water in our town tastes bad.

"Awww," I said.

"It sure ain't sorghum," said the Only Other Customer in Town, as he checked out *The Finer Techniques of Baking Beans*, *Lost Secrets of the Frijoles*, and *Phaseolus Vulgaris and You*.

Many of our townspeople thought that our water was piped directly from the River Acheron, a potent mix of sulfurous fumes licking wet, rusted nails. Whether the water was hot, or warm, or tepid, or even lukewarm varied widely, though it was usually warm. Recent changes in global climatic temperatures had not seemed to affect the water. The Biddies and the old-timers around of course thought that the water was fine. They invariably remembered it as cool and sweet, just as in their early years all the summers were sunny and good and all the winter months frigid with ten feet of snow. Biddies and cardboard-box shoes notwithstanding, the water in town had led some of our high school science teachers, and the majority of our town's thirty-seven clergymen, to speculate that:

and quite likely close to our town. It was a disturbing prospect; one made more disturbing by the agreement between Science and the Church. Fortunately, no one put much stock in what the preachers or the teachers had to say when it came to what we put into our mouths.

As I stood up from the water fountain, my face an iron pucker, a blue-gray shadow passed before my eyes. A Biddy stood just outside the library's heavy double doors.

"Aw, hell," I said.

"Row six hundred and sixty-six, sir," replied a skeletal librarian named Charon. "Way down in the basement."

"Oh. I really just wanted some earplugs," I said, as I paddled over to row seventeen with one less coin in my hand.

I walked down row seventeen and heard strange, muted laughter. The laughter stopped as I approached the earplugs. The earplugs sat nestled in between the poetry and the drama sections of row seventeen, where no one could find them. Our town had forgotten about poetry and drama. Row seventeen was a BBQ sandwich on a hieroglyphic map to Somewhere Else.

Sometimes townspeople would start down row seventeen, but then they would remember something else and go Away. Perhaps a new Tom Clancy book had arrived. Or Tony Hillerman passed through their mind like a cigarette. When this happened, Sam Shepard's books laughed at the other books in row seventeen like the offstage sound of a yelping coyote who had missed his dinner. William Stafford's cohorts, heedless of content, would then roll a few other books off the bookshelf onto the library carpet. The nearly complete and out-of-order works of Edward Albee lay in a cluttered pile in the middle row seventeen. Wallace Stevens' three books pretended that they were snowmen contemplating frost-encrusted boughs. The unopened hardbacks of Theodore Roethke danced a woeful waltz. The collections of Robert Frost and Thomas Hardy squeezed hard to keep Allen Ginsberg's oeuvre from joining the choir.

The lone book written by Lance Henson scowled at them all.

"It's a god-damn menagerie around here," said a fragile Tennessee Williams volume.

But the other books, which wore their covers like laughter-calluses, would ignore Sam Shepard's coyote-books, and row seventeen would quiet down again.

The earplugs never took part in the complicated dance of solitude played out between the unlikely partners: Poetry and Drama.

Standing on a copy of *The American Dream*, I selected a few packages of aqua blue earplugs from the cream-colored shelf. I would lay low until I was sure that the Biddy had left the scene. There were tables by a side window overlooking the library shrubs, so I took a seat. Graphite graffiti covered the tabletop.

Hours passed.

I smeared my fingers through pencil drawings of primitive genitalia; exact replicas of popular band logos; various crude, three-dimensional geometric shapes with plenty of extra lines; a plethora of:

banter; one Michelangelo-like prophet's early, misunderstood schematic for an engine of war; more genitalia; and numerous, indecipherable love notes.

I doodled myself.

I wrote half a poem. I tried to read. I looked through: two magazines on trout-fishing, one book on the symbiotic relationship between frogs and ponds, seven pamphlets ridiculing birth, four cooking magazines, one snowboarding magazine, three-quarters of a reference book on the archaeological history of the Meandering River, and one piece of scrap paper with cryptic numbers that may or may not have been encoded messages that lead one toward the publication of water, as subject, in one of its myriad and mysterious miasmas.

I sat at the dirty table and thought of band-aids and of blonde hair and of the failed romance of our small town lives.

I fondled my earplugs.

I wondered who put that cache of earplugs in row seventeen. It must have been long ago. Perhaps a guerilla faction of small-town, reactionary commandos that were finally tired of hearing it. Or maybe the earplugs were placed there by an otherwise kind librarian that just did not care for Sam Shepard's books.

I took a quick sniff. Then another, longer sniff. I sniffed. I snaffed. I snuffed. Only the dull, acrid scent of brimstone emanated from a nearby water fountain.

Biddy clear.

I checked out the packages of earplugs and high-tailed it home.

ON THE TRACKS WITH FRANK NORRIS' OCTOPUS

My Only Friend in Town and I walked the railroad tracks that night like plagiarism. We took along several bottles of white port wine.

"Congratulations, my friend," said My Only Friend in Town. "We've solidified our places as the 6,000,021th and 6,000,022th disenchanted youths to wind down the American Dream's creosoted tracks of yesteryear. Have a drink."

I took a drink.

"I remember one time out in Omaha our van got stuck waiting on a train," said My Only Friend in Town. "The train was long and seemed to stretch out for miles like Frank Norris' octopus and we missed our show."

"Oh," I said.

"Yeah," said My Only Friend in Town. "We went home after that." That old songwriting bug wormed through his brain. "When the caboose rolled by we all let out a sigh."

On the tracks, we imagined ourselves as footloose and fancy free spirits. Hobos. Beats. Caricatures of a curiously misplaced Americana. Riders on an imaginary range that we knew would end at home.

We did not mind.

We felt good about it, even if our ankles did hurt the next morning. At least we were going Somewhere Else.

We brought along plenty of Boredom Relief. The smoke wafted through the air and trailed in our wake like steam from a coal-fired engine.

My Only Friend in Town walked beside me in the dark and said, "This reminds me of this time I was playing in Albuquerque and saw the boxcars rolling down the line, and I thought that was cool, but then I realized that I should go and get some new guitar strings."

I tripped on a railroad spike that lay on top of the fist-sized chucks of limestone strewn about the railroad ties. The chunks of limestone were like a game of jacks. As I tripped, a vision of Lisa's tresses appeared before me in the darkness. The image wavered in the shadows—golden in the night—indistinct from the moon, and the dying trees, and the hushed peeping of the frogs.

I had always loved Lisa's hair. It flowed long and unadorned like waves in a perfect sea—O, to be a boat on that water! Lisa's hair haunted me the rest of that night—past the dogs barking, past the male bonding, past the fact that we turned back only six miles from town once the barking became berating, and past the fact that he was My Only Friend in Town and it was really late.

"Dude, you're 'hair'-brained," sang My Only Friend in Town. "You know, that might be a good idea for a song."

I took a long pull from the sweet, cheap wine.

"Hey, give me some more of that port."

"I've pulled into port and the destination is grim."

"I just got sick of it and gave up."

At that moment in the black night, as if they were referees blowing a whistle on our game of life, the dogs barked.

"BARK, BARK, BARK," said the dogs. "BARK!"

Short, rapid yelps like megaphones of cannon fire.

I dropped the bottle of white port wine, and it shattered on the game of jacks.

"Damn," I said.

"I christen thee 'Fucked,'" ordained My Only Friend in Town.

The black night looked blacker.

"We're pretty far from town," I said. "And it's really late."

"Dark," said My Only Friend in Town, displaying an acute level of acumen brought on by copious amounts of wine and generous tokes of Boredom Relief.

Six miles from home, on foot, widened into an ocean of space to our small-town, twenty-first century minds. We could have been on Another Planet, surrounded by Other Planet rocks of limestone and the dark side of nothingness. We could have been Somewhere Else, but we were not. Communication was down. Connection was lost. Cell phones had not yet reached our ears, nor would they for many years. There was no one to call anyway.

I would never hear them.

"BARK! BARK! BARK!" said a cannon-dog. "BOOM!"

In unison, we turned and ran for town. We stumbled on the oversized rocks and tripped on the ties in a wild, rambling spree of youth—suddenly full of laughter, and abandon, and thoughts that did not matter. Full of the blossom of spring, the scent of sex, the opening flower. Full of enough testosterone to lift a small car several inches off the ground or to burn an old couch in the middle of the street. Full of life. Full of the will to be more.

Full of shit.

Then: between the shining tracks, a whiff of perfumed residue. The bitter smell transmogrified into a bodice of black lace. Our nostrils filled with terror. We were trapped, five and a half miles out.

"Whatcha' doin' boys?" the Biddy creened.

"AHHHHHHHH!"

"Kind of late for bein' away—so late?" the Biddy asked, as if she were Sir Arthur Conan Doyle and the Curse of the Big Stench.

I concentrated on my earplugs. Gyrations began. Woozy from the intense blast of Eau de Auld, or more likely from the wine, I fell into reverie: Lisa.

"DAMN, THAT STINKS!" said My Only Friend in Town.

In the shadows of the Long Gone Railroad Company's legally

stolen land, sheer stillness prevailed.

A cricket chirped, though I did not hear it.

"Chirp," said the cricket.

My Only Friend in Town said, "I put no worth in bright and shiny things."

The Biddy stared at him with the eye of a crow.

"Just out lookin' for my dog again. Runs off every night," she said. With that, the Biddy drifted away like a black balloon off-gassing into the night—mysterious and empty.

"What did she say?" I throbbed, not hearing anything but the wind between my earplugs. My abridged History of Mad Sex with Lisa Reverie had come and almost gone.

My Only Friend in Town said, "Dude, you're such a boner."

O, fading memory of long blonde hair!

I looked around in the darkness of the tracks. I pulled my earplugs out and took in a long, deep breath of the blackest night air. A cool breeze swooped into my ear canals, and I shivered. The Biddy's putrid essence lingered in a creosoted bubble about our bodies, a siren song beckoning us toward home.

"Let's go home," said My Only Friend in Town.

I pushed the earplugs deep into my ears.

The hobo had died.

Eau de Auld remained.

There was no hope, and it was dark.

THE RABBITS

Not far from the Round House, four hundred yards up the Old I.C. Road, the small, popular, but not-quite-thriving Meandering River Livery eeked out business in an unkempt shack on the side of the road. The shack stood just off the highway, as if it were an unsuccessful hitchhiker who had been awaiting a ride out of our town for the past thirty-three years, but in the meantime had decided to make what he could of a bad situation.

A host of musty faded-orange life jackets, oars of all sizes, used plastic suntan lotion bottles, and a vast array of snack-wrapper trash littered the grounds around the shack. Red, green, and yellow downturned canoes and kayaks lay everywhere. Painted on each kayak and canoe was the Livery's motto:

Many of the canoes lay stacked at intervals on modified livestock trailers. The trailers were attached to old, beat-up conversion vans, ready to be hauled to one of the Livery's three drop-off points alongside the river.

The Meandering River Livery catered to tourism. Tourists came in from Somewhere Else and spent thirty dollars to rent a canoe, drink beer, and get sunburned. While they waited for the van, their children listened to terrifying stories of the Rabbits. As the stories went, the Rabbits arose from the river to wreak havoc on ill-fated boaters and their poor, helpless, and unable-to-swim-for-it children. White, frothy, and prone to be loud, the Rabbits were rumored to have swept lifevest-less children into the deepest depths of the river's channel, leaving nothing but insubmersible plastic oars and bobbing silver beer cans in the churned-up wake.

The Meandering River Livery: cottage industry seed of Tourism.

Out on the river, soft-shell turtles plopped into the river around the passing canoes, and common watersnakes stared like Alaskan iron at the approach of more Loud People.

"Here come some more Loud People," burbled a turtle.

"I hate you," hissed a snake.

"Hey look! A snake!" yelled the Loud People, very loud.

I went to the Livery every third day that had a two in the date's number, but only from July through warm days in September. This routine accounted for plenty of soggy shoes. The sand ground into the soles of my feet like a Grape-Nut going down the wrong way. I developed a perfect J-Stroke and strong arms, and I would think about our town and about Lisa in the dappled sunlight that would spill down through the early morning trees and then onto the smooth river like a haiku poem concerning falling petals and time.

I did not hear the Loud People.

I never missed them.

SAME OLD BLUES

I stayed at home to sleep or to watch the birds through my front window many days following Lisa. The birds would peck at remnants of sunflower husks that had sat in the trough of my little wooden bird feeder for weeks. The husks were lost David Attenborough episodes of survival and escape. Grackles and blue jays fighting for territory. Finches and cardinals accepting the leftovers. Mourning doves, mourning doves, mourning doves. The obligatory white-breasted nuthatch, the legions of house sparrows. Chickadees. On occasion, a red-bellied woodpecker would show up like changing TV stations to a good movie or to a program with attractive women that all resembled Lisa, but without pink headbands.

They never stayed for long.

On days full of rain, I sat around and tried to play folk songs. I envisioned other places and other sounds that did not seem so damning. Sometimes I would try to sing. I would pluck at my cheap brown guitar with its four rusted strings and a broken tuning peg. I would pretend that I was My Only Friend in Town in some lost city between Somewhere and Nowhere Else. On this fantastic stage, I could not hear our town. Its weight lifted from my shoulders. Its smells drifted Far Away. In the smoky crowd of my dream, Lisa swooned to my every word as I sang, and played, and made everyone happy in that indie sort-of-way that tried but did not succeed in actual happiness.

But husks did not nourish.

The birds would fly from my window.

Through my earplugs, the muffled tones of a fire engine roared through our town. My fingertips hurt from the metal strings of the guitar. I placed the guitar back behind my stereo and waited for the nuthatches to return, as the rain raced to the river, the Meandering River, which ran through our town.

Q-TIPS

Eventually, my soul grew tired from moping around the house. A fever descended upon my head.

I had begun to think about again going over to the Round House for a visit. I needed a break from bird watching. House sparrows and cardinals could only be fooled for so long. Then that old daemon, Fever, began tickling my throat, and inside my brain, and especially inside my ears. The lymph nodes in my neck swelled up to the size of green peas and then to the size of marbles and then to the size of jaw breakers. I realized that I had a problem.

Outside my trailer, our town pulsed like a heartbeat.

The sounds slow and faint.

My eardrums loud and negative.

I kept my earplugs in my ears and refused to accept the need for help.

My Only Friend in Town came over to see me, but I did not want to see him.

"C'mon man. Open the door," pleaded My Only Friend in Town.

I could not even hear him.

"You're like deaf but in reverse with those earplugs," My Only Friend in Town complained to my front door. "It's pretty annoying."

The sickness pervaded my entire body like an ocean of confusion. My Only Friend in Town had long gone Away. My ears began to tingle and to feel like a Q-Tip might do some good.

In the hallway, I uncorked the earplugs from my ears like an anti-celebration and reached for a blue box of Q-Tips. The Q-Tips sat beside a stack of worn-out bath towels and a bottle of pink calamine lotion. I swabbed through enough Q-Tips to wonder how many swabs it would take to throw the excessive-wax to healthy-oil ratio inside my ears into truly bad times. After the seventy-eighth Q-Tip from the blue box of 625, I had my answer. My ears had become tapped-out deserts of oil-less waste.

O, desert sands, blow not into my ears!

Itching, burning, bleeding: I still could not hear; the problem grew.

I called My Only Friend in Town.

He came over, reluctantly leaving a good video game, and looked into my ears with a flashlight.

"Gross," he said.

Continuous long-term earplug use had formed a dense ball of hard wax deep inside each of my ear canals. The natural waxplugs, like paraffin dams holding back the waters of my aqua blue earplugs, had nearly stopped up my ears completely. Only a minimum of sound flowed over each brown, waxy dam. This was a condition not at all helped by fervent Q-Tipping.

"Dude, your ears are really raw," sang My Only Friend in Town. "You should try some honey and herbal tea. That might help."

I began to fall down. Infections ensued; the fever raged. The human ear controls equilibrium and balance like a tightrope walker on the rope of sanity, and I was in the net.

I decided to visit the Hippie Store.

THE HIPPIE STORE

The Hippie Store was not well liked in town. Dirty, over-priced, and full of exotic groceries like baba ghanoush and umeboshi paste, miso and goat cheese, organic soap and pumpkin butter — not many of our townspeople dared darken its paisley door. There was the smell: the Hippie smell. Clove cigarettes, patchouli oil, stale beans. Rancid coffee in bulk and rotting drums of briny black olives. Turning mustard greens and shitake mushrooms. A general reeking of sin and abandon, left-wing conspiracies, and far-out thinking capped by a touch of burnt sweetgrass.

Hippie ying and Biddy yang.

I ran into the Hippie Store and knocked over a stack of sale-priced herbal tea boxes in the shape of a power-pyramid.

"Sorry . . . where are your ear candles?" I asked the scowling hippie clerk.

She pointed an aloof finger toward the Stay Dirty But Smell Good Section. The ear candles sat positioned on a top shelf alongside fluoride-free tubes of fennel-flavored toothpaste, loofahs, and indoctrinated bottles of Magic Soap. The ear candles gleamed down from above, and I took them in hand like salvation.

"I'll take these, please," I said to the clerk. A stockpile of vitamins, supplements, tinctures, and more vitamins upon vitamins proclaimed HEALTH THROUGH ADDITIVES IS THE NATURAL WAY.

The clerk rang up the ear candles. They cost a fortune. She scowled. Everything in the Hippie Store cost a fortune. The Hippie Store was like a socialist experiment in failure and a future filled with higher prices.

"Those ear candles cost a fortune," I said.

The clerk went back to reading her stolen copy of *What Is To Be Done?*

The Only Other Customer in Town stared at me as he grabbed a loaf of moldy black bread from a shelf.

I left the Hippie Store tripping on boxes of stale green tea and De-Tox that lay scattered about the floor like the vision of an acid trip gone bad.

I smelled like goat cheese for weeks. I could not wash off the scent, even with Magic Soap.

"Dude, you smell like ass!" brayed My Only Friend in Town.

Back home, My Only Friend in Town lit a match, and we burned the ear candles. What came out was not pretty. A river of dark orange torment flowed from my ears, and our small town screamed back in. My resolve was restored.

"Dude! Gross!" sang My Only Friend in Town in a high

falsetto with feeling.

"Yeah . . . I'm going to go get some more earplugs," I said.

"I wore earplugs one show we played," said My Only Friend in Town, "and it totally sounded quiet. I couldn't hear anything, and it didn't feel like we rocked. It's like, if it's too loud, you're too old."

I went out for more earplugs.

EARPLUGS

NATURE'S COURSE

Like an ancient reptile crawling on the beach of tomorrow, I headed to the library to restock my earplug larder.

A haze of Eau de Auld hung over our town. Biddies moved up and down the sidewalks in crotchety lockstep. No one but the occasional tourist could be seen. Dim shadows of town denizens flitted here and there behind thin checked curtains, their windows sealed tight.

"I really need some more earplugs," I said.

I slithered into the library and headed for row seventeen. Sam Shepard's books perked up their papery ears. An Albee book hit the floor. Sam Shepard's books glanced at the lonesome book by Lance Henson and hoped for better days.

"I heard John le Carré's new book is in," Lance Henson's book whispered.

Sam Shepard's books stifled a collective chuckle, fodder for the next harangue against row seventeen. But the other books in the row, whose spines were still stiff and neatly uncreased, remained stoic and unmoved.

I grabbed four packages of aqua blue earplugs and walked

over to the Stolen Books Section of the library. The Stolen Books Section consisted of seven rows of ceiling-high, cream-colored metal bookcases in various states of repose without books. The library wanted to illustrate the number of books that were never returned. The Stolen Books Section comprised approximately one quarter of the library's floor space and was constantly monitored by three high school age library volunteers. The volunteers all wore glasses and slacks and looked very busy. Sometimes, they rearranged the missing ghost books into a new system of order that acknowledged the fundamental flaws in the Dewey Decimal System, as if the Dewey Decimal System were mathematics, or religion, and the high school volunteers scions of revolution. Other times, the volunteers simply dusted the shelves.

"Excuse me," an attendant high schooler said, as he dusted an empty spot on the shelf where a missing copy of *The Shining* should have been placed. "Can I help you?"

"I'm looking for a book," I said.

"This is the Stolen Books Section," he dusted. "The books in the Stolen Books Section aren't here. They're stolen. Perhaps you should try the On-Hold Section or maybe the Missing Books Catalogue. I'm sure you can find what you're looking for Somewhere Else."

I affixed a fresh set of earplugs into my ears and looked around and out the library windows to the bright sunny day. I walked outside and stood on the broken sidewalk. The town spun slowly about like a carousel. Old farmers twirled hopelessly around and around. Town churches intoned the hour. Gravitational energy radiated outward and back inward in a perfect, balanced state of equilibrium. The sound still deafened.

Somewhere on those sidewalks, Lisa ran.

Away.

I decided to visit a favorite place: the Back of the Lake.

THE BACK OF THE LAKE

It took a while to get to the Back of the Lake. But once there, I could smoke cigarettes and not worry too much about town. I often went out to the Back of the Lake with My Only Friend in Town, but my favorite times were when I was alone. Lisa and I had never gone out to the Back of the Lake. I could not see her dancing on the rotten picnic tables or splashing in the cold water near the fishhook-laden shore.

The Back of the Lake was quiet, but risky, too. Like a gauntlet of malicious eye-clubs, numerous houses lined the road that lead down to the Back of the Lake, which was preserved land—state land—and technically off-limits after dark. I took the missionary position. I drove as carefully as could be between these homes until I reached the parking lot and the hallowed shores of the water. Twelve picnic tables sat upon the Back of the Lake's grounds. Trash spilled everywhichway. Raccoons skulked in the weeds. Opossums hid in their dens. The stars were bright and teemed with pregnancy.

"Boy, it sure is great here," I sighed, as a noxious cloud of cigarette smoke spewed from my lips.

"Loud people," grumbled a raccoon.

The Back of the Lake's boundary abutted an unincorporated section of our county. The boundary was divided like scissors in the hands of a child: willfully and succinctly. The citizenry could no more encroach upon the public land which bordered the public water than a convict could swim the seas of sin to freedom. The last house which bordered the lake's grounds had only half a shed. The other half was missing, cut off by order of the State Bureaucracy for the Maintenance of Public Grounds (S.B.M.P.G.). The shed had been built a little too carelessly close to the property line, and now a daytime visitor to the Back of the Lake could plainly see dusty children's toys, license plates with incomplete numbers, sawed-off gardening implements, and random used and unused automobile parts through the open and missing half of the shed. Sometimes the owner of the house could be seen mowing his yard with only half of a once whole lawnmower, patiently trimming his grass only halfway at a time.

I smoked cigarettes at the Back of the Lake when it was cold, or when the weather was otherwise inclement and there was no one else around. I liked to feel the biting chill and the harsh wind blowing across the lake's waters, the sting of frost on my cigarette fingertips. At night, the stars would shine, and I would be reminded that the lake was man-made and therefore not quite right, but still peaceful in its way. A mystery. A forgotten economic stimulus package of outdated tourism. A part of the town, yet not part of the town. A small body of fetid water infused with drowned fence lines, eminent domain, catfish, lost swimming holes, and lost dreams—the odor of Eau de Auld and the Biddies dampened by the rank weeds and the dead fish smell of the lake.

I smoked my cigarette and shivered. I got back in my car and drove the back roads of the county. I would drive until it was time to go home and to sleep in my bed and then to wake up again. I thought about masturbation and Lisa like symptoms of our town.

I saw deer and they ran.

Away.

OTHERS' ORIGIN

My Only Friend in Town said, "Man, drinking alcohol is like forgetting your place on earth. Which way is north?"

I tried to orient myself with town, but My Only Friend in Town and I were out in the woods. I could only see distant trees, and hills, and the blinking red lights of radio towers, which were not much help at all.

The taste of the Salsa Vendor's Pole Star Salsa flooded my taste buds, but gave me no indication of my whereabouts.

"On tour we didn't even use a map," bellowed My Only Friend in Town. "We just looked *around*."

I looked around. I thought perhaps that I could find a tree with moss growing on one side. I could not remember which side the moss grew on that would indicate direction. I walked over to a gnarly-barked old oak tree. A big black ant crawled along the ridges and furrows of the gray, moss-flecked bark. The bark seemed as if it were its own beautiful cosmos and the ant a giant, mythical traveler on the Great Constellation of Life.

I stared at the ant and the tree and time passed slowly.

"Cardinal directions are meaningless," sang My Only Friend in

Town. "I mean, people are smiling, and we can meet people from others' origin."

"Others' origin?"

"Yeah."

I thought about what he said for eighteen and a half seconds. I decided that I would never eat psychedelic mushrooms again.

My Only Friend in Town said, "History is written by the winners, and I'm not sure that I'm not a slave."

"Hey, let's go camping," I suggested.

"Alright," said My Only Friend in Town.

We plotted our trip by looking at more trees.

We stumbled from the woods and drove north or south into town. Once inside the perfumed clutch of our municipal confines, we dodged Biddies and headed over to the shady side of town, which was very close to the poor people.

"I need some more orange juice," requisitioned My Only Friend in Town.

We pooled the money that we had into a mutual camping fund: forty-nine dollars and seventeen cents. We spent the majority of this buying another baggie of Boredom Relief, so that we would not be bored. The rest of the money we saved for food supplies and other knickknacks. Little remained. We needed to scrounge up more change.

"Hey! I found another dime!" celebrated My Only Friend in

Town. He triumphantly pulled a gooey-haired dime from deep inside his couch cushions. His couch was like a filthy piggy bank with a nearly inexhaustible supply of disgusting coins. "Maybe we can get some Boston Baked Beans!"

"I need a new sleeping bag," I said.

I drove my fist deep into the piggy bank couch.

It was close to the weekend, and we were going camping.

THE SERVICE INDUSTRY

My Only Friend in Town and I decided to wait and to camp out on Saturday night. We needed to mine a few more coins from the couch. We needed to buy a new sleeping bag and to ready our souls for another good time. But on Friday morning, with our provisions nearly secured, heavy clouds billowed in a roiling sky. Rain showers loomed in our brains as if we were soggy French bread pirates adrift in cavernous bowls of onion soup with way too much pepper.

"Ahoy!" I said.

"Bail out the scurvy lines!" screamed My Only Friend in Town, in his best impression of a buccaneer with no lemons.

"I better check the paper," I said.

My Only Friend in Town slurped, coughed, and sputtered, "Good idea, *mon ami*."

I looked up the weather forecast in our town's newspaper, the *Local Daily*. The weather section consisted of three color symbols that stood for: Today, Tonight, and Tomorrow. The symbols had not changed since the *Local Daily's* first run of *Barney Google and Snuffy Smith* long ago. The sun symbol always wore a smile, and the cloudy symbol a frumpy frown. The moon symbol was invariably small and yellow and shaded according to its stage. Old Man Winter took the part of a windy day and blew a frosty curl of lines from his dour, puckered mouth. Save for our town's three-symbol forecast, no regional, state, or national weather projection was ever mentioned in the *Local Daily*. An op-ed writer from the Next County Over once mentioned that it was hot there. This proclamation set off a thunderstorm of speculation in town concerning our foul, and often warm, water.

I flipped through the six pages of our paper and found the weather section next to an advertisement for the Good Grouse Bed and Breakfast. Saturday wore a smile. Our worries were assuaged like sausage and anagrams in a screenplay by Will Shortz with all the answers. We quickly made plans to pitch our camp in the woods by a little creek. The creek had multiple tributaries that we would have to cross and to re-cross several times like a crossword puzzle to reach our campsite. The would-be camp lay nestled in a little floodplain between two small hills where the tourists would never find us.

I had not been camping for years.

"I haven't been camping for years," I said.

"Sometimes I just play a song in my head," rehearsed My Only Friend in Town, "and it sounds just like the record."

"I like to wear these earplugs," I said.

Dark clouds swept across the sky. Eau de Auld swirled in the wind.

I thought about baguettes and about canned baked beans and about how the woods had been taken over by our mayor, the Service Industry.

The Service Industry had grown up in town. She blossomed into an upstanding citizen at an early age. Gaining power, as one does in our town, through extensive administrative work in the public school system followed by low-level civic service and adroit marital choices, the Service Industry had made a run for the mayor's office six years ago and succeeded.

Upon entering office, the Service Industry implemented Tourism, and our town prospered. Gone were unpaved trails into nature's scenic wonderland and in were paved, handicap-accessible mini-roads and trash. Gone were wooden pit-toilets and in were concrete pit-toilets. Cheap, unimproved land full of the Biddies' progeny vanished and up popped the Nestled Inn, Our Little Cabin, the Good Grouse Bed and Breakfast, and hundreds of government-sponsored State Forest cabins with tin roofs the color of money.

A fragile relationship borne of greed, political savvy, real estate, and cheap groceries developed between the Service Industry and the Biddy Brigade. Though the Biddies devastated municipal commerce with their hateful stench, they had boon years in the boondocks as county land prices increased. State funds poured in. The Biddies' homegrown Mom and Pop Country Stores thrived out on county lands.

Tourism flourished.

"Hey, we need to buy some toilet paper and bug spray and some of those pre-packaged, plastic-wrapped things of firewood," a tourist might have said. "Maybe they have some up at that Mom and Pop Country Store there."

"Get some hot dogs, too."

The Service Industry lurked in her sweltering office. With a shoo-in re-election to a second term, she was handed *carte blanche* keys to the front door of our town. She implemented her master plan after a hardy pancake breakfast at the Lions Club: *Tourism II, and the Big Box Descendeth*. The plan shot across the bow of the Biddies' orange pontoon boat.

The need for cheap goods continued to increase in the outlying areas of our county: Biddy territory. The Service Industry forced Town Council's hand to expand the town limits and to give massive tax breaks to new businesses on the freed-up land. Trees fell. Dirt moved. The Biddies were furious. They lost significant chunks of prime, unincorporated land. They lost a fortune in revenue from their Mom and Pop Country Stores. Tourists flocked to the newly built Cheap Foreign Goods (C.F.G.) supercenters with shelves like Christmas.

The old gave way to the new.

"I can even get some new socks," a tourist said. "And a rotisserie chicken!"

Our town grew like a thousand suckling ticks on a thousand hairy hearts.

The Biddies wanted some of the blood.

ROOTS

My Only Friend in Town said, "You can take the boy out of a small town, but you can't take the small town out of a boy."

He always said things.

Like that.

LIKE ROTTING PUMPKINS IN A NOVEMBER FIELD

The Service Industry grew up in town, but her family went only a generation back. This had given the Service Industry a particular lack of clout as she climbed our town's socio-political ladder into a mature forest of family trees. The roots of many of these trees, despite the hard clay and the general lack of topsoil in our county, ran deep. Certain town-specific family names went eight or more generations back, often with county road names to prove it. The many limbs, forks, deadfalls, branches, and general lack of pruning created a social hierarchy that was both complex but well understood. Only the freshest transplants to town were sometimes confused. These transplants usually did not last very long. They withered and died from a lack of fertile jobs, or social connection; they moved Far Away.

The Service Industry, though still growing roots, had nevertheless become firmly entrenched in the sub-stratum of our town's soil with her second elected mayoral term. Her undying town loyalty—she wore our high school colors every Friday without fail during football season—her local marriage, her devout patriotism, her religious piety, and her clear understanding of the finer workings of small-town politics enabled her to spread her will like the taproot of a hardy and successful weed invasively sweeping through the forest of our town.

"Probably *Ailanthus altissima*," classified one of our high school science teachers. "Yes, highly invasive. The seeds! The SEEDS!"

Of course, the Service Industry was still susceptible to the Long Vines of Endless Gossip; everyone was. But there was no denying a two-term mayor was part of the town. The profit-driven motivational force she propagated through Tourism worked like a rototiller on virgin soil. Her first-generation status was over. Town Council had even petitioned to have the new road out by the C.F.G. named Service Industry Way in her honor.

There was no longer a question of where the Service Industry was from; she was from our town.

The Service Industry's family moved to town just prior to her birth. Like many newcomers, they fit the Three Requirements of Town Immigration. Her parents where:

1) from Somewhere Else

2) about to have a kid and

3) looking for a cheap, quaint place to raise their child as far from Hell, the Big City, or the-Small-Town-of-Their-Youths as they could find.

They had not yet tasted our water; they had no roots. If they had, they probably would have gone back to them. Instead, they moved in from Somewhere Else like out-of-town tourist hunters, who increasingly descended on our pretty, bountiful county every fall as visions of a Big Buck danced in their heads.

People in town still clung to past precedent on the matter, but the policy of Tourism had effectively reduced the Three Requirements of Town Immigration to a single requirement:

1) from Somewhere Else.

Council, shaking off years of overt political dust, passed a resolution in favor of the change, and the Service Industry clapped. Virtually overnight, new cultural customs, regional dialects, the same bland foodstuffs, different civically-honored surnames, camouflage pants, self-aggrandizing brochures, and blaze orange vests erupted like chicken of the woods mushrooms all around our rotting town and our decaying county. The Only Other Customer in Town suddenly disappeared, nowhere to be found. Unlike the newcomers, who were here to stay, the hunters brought nice-looking vehicles with extended trailers and mud-splattered ATV's, which rolled through our town and then out again with corn-fed deer carcasses strapped to their clean, waxed roofs. Dead deer tongues lolled and wagged in the breeze and said such things as:

"Crap, I'm venison."

Or, "I hope they don't jerk me."

Or sometimes, if it was a particularly vain dead trophy buck, he would say, "All I can do is hang my head."

Like our bricks, coal, wood, and the rare Olympic-caliber high school basketball player, most of the deer harvest would leave the county for destinations Elsewhere.

But the forests grew back, the deer were plenty, and the hunters flocked in: Tourism.

The Salsa Vendor, sensing opportunity like the prospect of land at sea, salsaed in on the action. He turned capitalist, got a small business loan with help from the new, not-for-profit Building a Better Place Initiative, and began marketing a special end-of-the-garden line of salsas: the Late Season Special, the Butternut Squash Experience, the Salsa Venture, the Deer Steak Meltdown, and the exceptional One Flew Over the Tomatillo. Each jar was hand-packed, seasonal, and labeled with a blaze orange and camo decal. He could not manufacture them fast enough.

"I still prefer the piccalilli," recorded the clerk of courts.

"Piccalilli?" said a hunter.

As Tourism boomed, our hills became increasingly more inviting. Land prices skyrocketed; immigration was up. Town Council, spurred into action by their immigration policy success, passed pertinent resolutions for the first time in decades. New town ordinances multiplied like fishes and loaves in the hands of many small-town Jesuses. Biddy patrols decreased. The Service Industry called for the reinstatement of the Last Police Chief in Town, and he said that he would think about it.

"I'll think about it," said the Last Police Chief in Town.

Geologically-indiscriminate, time-saving roads were built as quickly as the trees would come down, new homes could go up, and certified modern gas-station convenience stores could service them.

"I remember this time I walked over there where that new gas station is now," said My Only Friend in Town, "and I thought that the trees looked really nice beside that creek with the aluminum-tainted water. There was a soft murmurous sound from the leaves, and I thought that was pretty cool even though it wasn't applause."

"That water was kind of gross though," I said, absentmindedly pushing an earplug.

"I'm pretty sure it was from an old mine."

"I also think it was actually pretty loud and not so soft and so murmurous," I continued, pushing harder on my earplug, as our town leaked in.

"Yeah, it was," said My Only Friend in Town. "But that's all gone now. Well, except for the creek and for that aluminum-tainted run-off."

A few months later, my earplugs temporarily broke down and I heard through the Long Vines of Endless Gossip that Lisa got a job at that same Travel Center Gas Station and liked it. She began dating. She met her future husband, the son of a Biddy, in the Travel Center's Ice Cave Beer Cooler while stocking six-packs of cheap, domestic, high-powered Boredom Relief. In future years, with the experience she gained at the cash register and with the help of Tourism, Lisa turned this position of social contact into a full-fledged run at Head Biddydom. After her marriage, Lisa effectively took over management of all seven of the Biddies' Mom and Pop Country Stores. The other Biddies did not mind; they were old. Lisa melded her past know-how of the inner workings of a corporate service station with the small-fry, socially-entrenched successes of the Biddies' Mom and Pop Country Stores, went public with them, and succeeded. Lisa and her man bought one of the large, brand new homes built just outside town, made money hand over fist, and lived happily ever after on Tourism, roller dogs, a mediocre health insurance policy, and an over-abundance of kids. Her husband took up golf and never worked another day in his life. The Ole Homestead became Her New House.

"Fore!" yelled that son of a Biddy.

"I hate that guy," I said.

Lisa never ran again.

Commerce inoculated our town like exotic shitake mushroom spores in a felled local oak log. Where once were just rolling hills, now baby towns, flea markets, Amish furniture outlets, and roadside vegetable stands sprouted up by the new roads, intersections, and gas stations, all attempting to monopolize on Tourism as Growth and Prosperity.

"Incorporate them!" screamed the Service Industry.

Tax money flowed into town like a spring flood into the homes of the still-poor.

Our town had not seen a boom like this since the Coal Days of yesteryear.

But most of our town was yesteryear. Our town's old families had lived through the Fall of Coal, and our roots had not yet been forgotten.

Exploitation.

The Service Industry loved it.

"Growth and prosperity," plotted the Service Industry. "That's what our town needs. And if we have a new town when it's all said and done—then so be it. The old town was old."

The Service Industry would often stand at the edge of town, or down by the Bait and Guns Shop, wearing Carhartt overalls and a blaze orange hunting jacket. She looked exactly like a stale leftover Halloween shortbread pumpkin cookie with orange and brown icing, except that the Service Industry was made of flesh and bone and was not made of cheap white cake flour and hydrogenated vegetable oil. She would stand there and wave and greet the tourist hunters as they came into town to fill up the municipal coffers on guns, ammo, and grease. Tourism hung like an umbrella above her.

Winds blew. Rain fell. Skies darkened. The Biddies stunk. The Service Industry stood unmoved: the stale cookie with a jack-o'-lantern smile.

"You boys be careful now," she would meticulously call out to a group of out-of-town nimrods, as they picked up a box of one-ounce shotgun slugs, a sack of hamburgers, and a six pack of suds. "Hope you get a big one!"

"Yes, ma'am," the men would reply, "we sure will."

Our town reeked of incoming Commerce like deer scent around a corn feeder. Above it all loomed the Service Industry, watching adroitly from her tree-stand office, or from down on the edge of town.

"She's like Annie Oakley up there," said My Only Friend in Town, "hovering over the killing fields of our town."

Far out in the county hinterlands, and very close to the Ole Homestead, the Biddy Brigade was at work. As gunfire erupted about them in our multi-colored autumnal hills and jubilant hunters tagged deer, the Biddy Brigade labored, cutting and discarding long worthless strips of venison leg and skull. As they worked, the Biddies munched on the deer's tarsal, metatarsal, and pre-orbital scent glands as if they were Boston Baked Beans. A good number of the Biddies' offspring processed deer carcasses for both the tourist and the townie hunters alike, and this year the offal went straight to the Biddies' new operation: Project Auld.

"Got another load, Mom."

The glands crunched in the Biddies' mouths like footsteps on dried fallen leaves; the smell of Pyrodex and something new was in the air.

"Save some for the pot, now. Save a few back for the pot," stank the Head Biddy.

And in they went.

Odeur Nouveau was on the fire.

THE SLEEPING BAG

I needed a decent sleeping bag before heading out on our camping trip, so My Only Friend in Town and I crossed the Mighty Bridge and walked to the north side of town and our dying strip mall.

"I know just the place," I said. Sporting Goods and Hardware, aisles ten and eleven.

"Right over here, sir," said the clerk. "But I'm all out of apples."

"That's OK," I said. "Rather than bearing some fruit, perhaps you could just show me your sleeping bags."

"Well, OK," said the clerk.

The clerk walked over to an assortment of sleeping bags curled up like plastic-wrapped grub worms and peeled one off the shelf.

"This one's pretty decent," he said.

The advertisement on the sleeping bag said:

"Hmmm," I said.

"It's cheap," said the clerk.

"OK," I said.

"If you wear extra clothes at night, you should be pretty well off in these temperate rolling hills if you ever decide to make camping a hobby rather than an excuse," said the clerk.

I walked out of the store with the sleeping bag five minutes later.

"These nickels are disgusting," said the cashier.

Signs hung all around Sporting Goods and Hardware advertising "Our Last Two Legs Discount Sale," so My Only Friend in Town picked up new camping pots and plates and cups for one dollar apiece. Then he saw the wine bota. The bota was made of red plastic and imitation leather with a thin veneer of real cowhide for authenticity. My Only Friend in Town imagined that he would like to drink sweet port wine from that bota. He also imagined that he would like to say funny things such as "Go man go!" or "Spid-lee doo-de de!" and spray long streams of wine down his throat as if he were a Beatnik wannabe in a dusty, open-bed truck in far off sunny old Somewhere.

"I got some cups and plates and pots," said My Only Friend in Town, as he walked out of the store. "And a bota."

"I got a new sleeping bag," I said.

Our gear complete and our money all but spent, we were almost ready to head for the hills. But first, we needed a night of rest.

"I'm hungry," I said.

"We need some Friday night pizza."

"I think this sleeping bag's pretty decent," I said.

"Trainstop Pizza," said My Only Friend in Town.

PIZZA

My Only Friend in Town and I ordered a pizza—half pepperoni and cheese and half the works minus anchovies—from Trainstop Pizza on the east side. Trainstop was the longest-standing pizza joint in town and our favorite among the fourteen new pizza parlors that had popped up like churches in the wake of our town's past socio-economic downturn. New pizza shops, both corporate and cottage, continued to pop up with the rise of the Service Industry and Tourism. Steeples and pepperoni made no distinction when it came to human weakness: a small slice of heaven or a hot piece of pie—the dough was all the same.

"It's strange how pizza and religion both carry the weight of the poor," re-marxed My Only Friend in Town.

Prior to Tourism, the boom years in town ended about a hundred years ago. During that time, the majority of cost-effective natural resources had been thoroughly gleaned from our then-not-so-pretty-looking-hills of yesteryear. Deforestation was a chic look in turn of the century America. The hills looked somewhat akin to Dr. Seuss's denuded Truffala landscape of post-Once-ler stumps in *The Lorax*, a book which was currently missing from our library.

The gluttonous frenzy was brought on by the usual things. War. Greed. The insatiable human need for Growth. A symbolic, bald-eagle-taloned handful of coal and of dust and of wood and of iron thrown straight into the fiery furnace of the Industrial Revolution and cooked until well done. The result left our once beautiful, tree-covered hills as bare and scorched as the California countryside amid rising global temperatures and failed forest protection policies that all resulted in ugliness. SEE: *NAPALM BBQ*. But unlike the land of Steinbeck and roses, there was nothing left here to come back to. Pink headbands can wash Away. Mighty Bridges can crumble. Friends often do become memories. After the resources gave out, our town dried up like a worm on a sunny sidewalk, and Prosperity packed its gilded suitcase for finer pastures.

Only Appalachia and greenbriers remained.

So the state came in, and the government came in, and between them they bought up the clear-cut, mined-out land, gob piles and all. What was once owned by the people was now owned by the state. Trees began to grow; forests were named. Large tracts of state and national land coalesced and buffered our town from the outside world, new roads, and jobs. And Tourism, like a phoenix, lay in wait.

O, Tourism, born from the ashes of Greed.

"And greed is what I need like a thneed," sang My Only Friend in Town. "Get that pizza, man!"

I headed over to pick up the pizza.

As implied by its name, Trainstop employed a locomotive décor to sell pizzas. Old photographs of our town's history adorned the walls of the parlor, often featuring engines and boxcars and a hopeful, if tired, expression on the townspeople's faces. Flour mills, marching bands, doomed canals, and wistful horses stood in various frozen tones of sepia or gray and watched patrons eat pizza and drink warm draft beer or Pepsi throughout all the bustling business hours of time. RR Xing signs hung everywhere; and in an inspired, if obvious, stroke of marketing genius from the local management:

logos were stamped on innumerable pizza box tops, which were soon filled with Trainstop's special Railroad Penny pizzas and sent out for delivery like the Fireball Mail.

And as if our bodies were formed of daguerreotypes and acid baths, borne by failure and a need for a connection to the past — preferably marked by trains of some sort — we, the townspeople, flocked to Trainstop week in and week out. Trainstop was our modern-day train station, the cultural hub of our town. No one cared that our real train station out by the Long Gone Railroad had fallen down covered in vines. Most people in town had no idea that it was even there. Trainstop Pizza brought together tourist and townie, young and old, rich and poor, enemy and friend, and kneaded them like all-purpose dough under a baker's rough hands, until they co-mingled like yeast and flour, draft beer and pepperoni pizza, red pepper flakes and parmesan cheese, laughs, cries, coal, and fire on the Great Steam Engine of Time.

I walked in to pick up our pizza. In the back bar, next to the arcade games, the Only Other Customer in Town sat perched on a black-padded chrome stool sipping flat draft beer from a glass mug, like a hobo hugging a can of baked beans. Around him, punk kids banged away on pinball flipper buttons. The jukebox played the same outdated pop song that it had played for years. Pushy waitresses with faces like pizza dough picked up trays of beer and Pepsi and God help you if you bumped them. Antsy patrons waited close by for the-only-pisser-in-the-place, which nestled up against the farthest back corner of Retail Space Nowhere. They nonchalantly watched the blipping of the arcade games or the cute young behinds of the teenaged players. Trainstop was the Place, and hormones partied there like Dionysian feasts of renewal and, given our countywide teenage pregnancy rates, rebirth.

As generations of our town's framed forebears stared down upon him, the Only Other Customer in Town burped and said, "I love pizza."

I grabbed my Railroad Penny and left.

THE CAMPSITE

Dusk settled as My Only Friend in Town and I reached our campsite. It had taken a bit longer than expected to fill in the crossword puzzle path that brought us to our destination. We were still unsure of 6-Down. As we forded the last "A director with blind issues" creek and stepped over the final fallen "Zany comic book villain" log, shadows spilled over the leaves and the moss like dying batteries of daylight. Rainclouds had come and gone, and dusk descended like a cloak thrown over a mud puddle. We quickly set up the tent in a level place and looked for wood to burn.

"Did you bring the flashlight?" I asked.

"We only need the firelight," sang My Only Friend in Town. "It's like on stage when the house lights go down."

"Oh," I said.

The rain clouds returned. Our party began. It was Saturday, and I took out my earplugs.

My Only Friend in Town sat across from me around the fire and yelled, "I hate rabbits! I hate rabbits!" in a futile attempt to ward off the green-wood smoke that carried up into his face. My can of beans burbled in the hot coals. The paper label wrapped about the steel bean can blackened and emitted small Technicolor flames as the dyes and the glue charred into nothingness.

"Next time only get dead wood," I said. "Green doesn't burn, it smokes."

"Smoking is fine if it's green," said My Only Friend in Town, as he rolled a big log of Boredom Relief. His face was ghoulish in the firelight. Flame-shadows danced a pantomime of *Reefer Madness* on his pale, lurid skin.

My beans bubbled and said, "We're done." I squirted a stream of sweet port wine down my throat from the bota and tore a chunk of white bread from my French baguette as if the bread, the wine, the Lost Generation, and I had all kneeled down together for a suppertime communion—fine pieces of crust all shattered like exploded stars.

"Take, and eat, this is my Eu-crust, given for you . . ."

Rain began to fall.

The ground had been saturated for days from previous storms and took little time to swell. Our fire popped and smoked. Our eyes were round like new philosophies or childhood, and we talked against the falling drops as they wet our clothes and sputtered into the fire. We were not leaving. We carried on, heedless of the rain, which fell and moved and funneled down and over. The rain. The water. The future Meandering River.

Our chatter went and came and left and returned—a giant

circle of communication stumbling on bricks of word.

"The Endless Chatter of Meaning!" sang My Only Friend in Town, as a raindrop struck him in the eye.

"The Ceaseless Circle of Certitude!" I said, as my butt got wet.

Pools of water formed in low places like hydraulic insurrection. From the corners of our crazed eyes, we suddenly saw our tent rise up on a sheet of liquid flood like surface tension voodoo and float past our stupefied faces into the darkness beyond the smoking light of our fire.

"Dude, our tent just floated away!" cried My Only Friend in Town. "I can't believe it!"

I fell off my sitting log. I reached out to break my fall and felt a sharp sting into the pad of muscles below my thumb.

"Ow! Damn! Something just bit me!"

My Only Friend in Town looked at my hand and yelled, "Dude, your thenar eminence is swelling up! And our tent just floated away! AHHHHHHHHHH!"

I heard him crashing through the woods after that and screaming into the night like a banshee with a lost pet named Tent.

"TEEEEEEEEEENT!" he cried. "TEEENT! WHERE ARE YOU?!"

I gazed at my hand and saw two tiny red marks wreathed in a halo of swollen white skin. I imagined a subtle poison coursing through my veins like the dark cloud of embarrassment, or guilt, or perhaps a failed love that could just not be forgotten.

Spider bite.

Shit.

"I guess our tent was in a low place," I said, sure that I would die quite soon as the poison spread and our tent escaped. I drank my last gulp of sweet port wine and walked blindly off to the car. Still unable to decipher 6-Down, I tripped on fallen limbs, slid up muddy banks, and splashed all over like a twisted survival version of "Jingle Bells," but without the laughing and with mud instead of snow.

"TEEEEEEEEEEEEEEEENT!" cried My Only Friend in Town from somewhere back inside the darkness.

In the car, I replaced my earplugs, curled up in a ball in the backseat, and fell asleep, worried. In this fetal position, I quite closely resembled my plastic-wrapped grub worm sleeping bag, which I had left back at camp unwrapped and bobbing against a pawpaw sapling.

As I slept, the poison pulsed a hallucinatory beat through my skull and my bones, pounding and reverberating against my blue, wax-flecked earplugs. Soiled dreams caromed across my psychedelic brain sky and fluttered like ugly butterflies in a tortured ritualistic dance of primal venom. Meteors of baby spiders with Lisa's long blonde hair shot through my terrified lullaby mind. Images of town swept like a sea through my blood. Biddies screeched. The Service Industry wailed. The Salsa Vendor sold salsa. And the poison ran its course.

On and on the rain fell, carried away by the Meandering River, which ran through our town.

ODEUR NOUVEAU
AND THE BRICK FACTORY

With the success of *Tourism II, and the Big Box Descendeth*, the Service Industry increased her sway in the confines of both our town and our county. The smell of Eau de Auld still wafted about town, but the Service Industry's best friend, Fast Food, had begun to make plans. The Biddies' crooked backs were up against the metaphorical wall. Tourists, townies, and folks living in the county had begun One Stop Shopping in town, a crucial subsection in the Big Box manifesto. Hearts, minds, and profit were lost at the Biddies' Mom and Pop Country Stores. The Biddies did what they had to do. They could not content themselves with another Walk-A-Thon on Main Street. They streamlined nasal operations.

In a nefarious move to subjugate the remaining sectors of town slipping from their aged control, and to quash the rising tide of Service Industrial power, the Biddy Brigade began to leave sample packets of a new, foul-smelling odor all over our town: on countertops and on park benches, in magazines and in window displays, in gutters and at Leo's, in front of the Bait and Guns Shop, at the Ten Cent Diner and at Trainstop, at breakfast, at schools—

especially at the schools — and, most heinously, in the seed section of the Hardware Store. The Biddies had even dropped off four score packets at the Relics for All Purposes Store, completely baffling the clerks. The west side of town was particularly well-saturated. How the Biddies had managed to ford the river and to carry out their odor-bombing remained a mystery. They must have had help. Young, lithe runners of a new smell: runners like Lisa.

"Yep, they've pretty much left them all over the place," inspected the Last Police Chief in Town. "East, west, north, south — the town's pretty much covered."

"That smells good!" whiffed a little girl, wading in a storm drain.

Thousands of the packets lay strewn across town on our locally manufactured brick sidewalks like noxious confetti after one stinker of a parade. Beneath the packets, the bricks were stamped with the names of surrounding counties, or towns, or the tell-tale swirls and markings indicative of the brick's creator. These sidewalks had been neglected for years, many for decades. The remaining bricks rose and fell like an obstacle course with grass between its toes. Many were loose like teeth. Most of the bricks were worn and cracked, their manufacturers long since forgotten by all but a few local brickidopterists, or sly carpet-bagging entrepreneurs, or artists ready to capitalize on "Bricks as Tourism" (SEE: *TOURISM II: SUBSECTION 9ii-A*) But some of the bricks were stamped:

THE BRICK FACTORY

our town's old, home-fired brick.

During its heyday, besides bricks, the Brick Factory had produced three hundred local jobs, massive tax cuts for the rich owners, and clay sewer piping. Back then, the Brick Factory, like a heart, sat just to the left of the center of town. An industrial railway line of the Long Gone Railroad served the Factory exclusively. The line split the Factory grounds perfectly in two and, like an aorta, ushered clay pipe and bricks to all points Far Away.

It was the Age of the Brick Barons. During those prosperous and self-reliant times, the Brick Factory provided enough bricks in lieu of property-tax inducing legislation to line every sidewalk and to pave most of the roads in town, west side excluded. The Brick Factory also manufactured enough clay pipe to ferry enough raw sewage directly into the Meandering River, downstream. This widespread and regionally acceptable practice of shitting on the next town down continued unabated thoughout our time.

"Send it Somewhere Else!" ordered our ancient mayor, the Captain of Industry.

EARPLUGS

"Keep that poop flowing," directed the Service Industry. "Away."

But that age, unlike most of its bricks, had crumbled. The Brick Factory's Long Gone Railroad line was abandoned; our town had grown and shifted its allegiance to the blacktopped roads. Townspeople had forgotten the story of the *Three Little Pigs*. People did not need these bricks any more. Our town's heart was in another place: Tourism.

The Brick Factory now lay in ruins farther from the center of town, a sacred burial ground of what-used-to-be. Wreckage and dirt was its marker, asbestos and decay was its memory. The Factory's talismanic powers for Commerce had ebbed, sputtered, wheezed, and died. Still, no Councilman would legislate against it, no owner would improve it, no fool would buy it, and no citizen would traverse it. Even high schoolers in desperate searching need of a secluded place for Boredom Relief, sex, or graffiti avoided the Factory grounds.

The Service Industry planned to change all that. For in failure she saw promise, and in history she saw profit. She hummed the tune to "America the Beautiful" every time she thought of the old Brick Factory, and she felt good. Change would come.

In her bedroom, all by herself, the Service Industry said, "I'll build this empire brick by brick, even if they are all broken."

She really meant it.

"I'll mold this town like its bricky red clay," she said. "And what was once their pride, and then their failure, will be their pride again."

She was hard to argue with; she was the mayor.

The Brick Factory was now relocated next to the freeway and renamed the Clay Pipe Products & Manufacturing Company. Clay Pipe dithered on the outskirts of town like a feeble old man sitting on a bench at the Mall, tired from his morning walk around Consumerism. Assorted clay pipes stacked twelve feet high on seven and a half acres of tax-deductible land awaited phantom semi-rigs to arrive and to haul them away to Somewhere Else. In the meantime, Clay Pipe's thirty-three workers continued to make and to sell the occasional outdated clay sewer pipe for other outdated municipal sewer systems. Specialization was Clay Pipe's future like the roots of power are deep, and the operation survived. The plant sat with kilns ablaze, the town was proud, and the volume was minimal.

"Hey, grab one of those clay pipes off that big stack of clay pipe back there," piped the Clay Pipe foreman.

A worker pulled an old clay pipe off a twelve foot stack of clay sewer pipe and blew off the dust. "I guess we'll have to make another pipe," he said.

The clay pipes lasted for years. They were virtually indestructible underground.

But now the pre-pipe progeny of our county's abundant clay

mineral resources — bricks fired-cured in the deepest bowels of the old Brick Factory's sixteen kilns and aged for four generations against footfall, dog shit, and hard rubber tires — lay lined with a most unpleasant disturbance in our town's Force: Odeur Nouveau.

The Biddies were wise. Like rising steam from a black Avon cauldron, the packets they made contained a new smell. It was sweet. It was flowery. The girls liked it.

Odeur Nouveau had arrived.

TINCTURE

Bending down to the sidewalk, the Hippie Store clerk picked up a packet of Odeur Nouveau, ripped it open, and sniffed the air. "Whoa," she said, "some tincture."

Lazy

Downtown, the lazy waitress walked slowly into work. Under her generic tennis shoes, packets of Odeur Nouveau screamed for help.

"Help," said a packet of Odeur Nouveau.

The lazy waitress walked on.

She would get one later.

FEET

Striding out of the Mayor's Office after a highly successful conference call with a local developer and her friend, the Banking Industry, the Service Industry decided that she could go for a lunch of French fries and a cold glass of milk. On the ground at her patent leather feet, a solitary packet of Odeur Nouveau sat like the last unturned stone.

"Oh," said the Service Industry, "what's this?"

RUNNING

Lisa ran through town. Suddenly, she tripped and she fell, crashing onto the brick sidewalk.

"Damn!" said Lisa.

Around her, twenty-seven packets of Odeur Nouveau sparkled like perfumed silver.

Though she still had three packets at home, Lisa picked them all up and ran.

Away.

THE OLE HOMESTEAD

"Soon they shall all smell," hissed the Head Biddy, up in the Ole Homestead.

The Ole Homestead constituted the de facto headquarters for the Biddy Movement. The house sat on a lovely tract of tulip poplar and black walnut far out in our eroded, but fetching, second-growth hills. An orange-tainted creek, the sulfurous result of old mine run-off, ran close by the home. Various rusting automobiles, swing sets, and antiquated pieces of farm equipment were permanently bivouacked about the estate, as if field batteries in a protracted, perhaps never-ending, campaign. A number of additions had been added to the Ole Homestead over the years, as indoor plumbing and baseboard heating had made headway in the county. Around and against the home, a multitude of blue plastic tarpaulins were fitted over lean-tos, doghouses, and other ramshackle structures. The tarps flapped and cracked like standards in the Eau de Auld breeze. The Ole Homestead, once vaguely Saltbox in style, had served five generations of Head Biddies and a revolving cast of unruly children. Biddy-men were rarely seen at the Ole Homestead, and if they were, they never said much. Nevertheless, torches at the Ole Homestead were passed, scents were remembered, and time moved on.

Now, the Ole Homestead was packed. Biddies from all parts of the county had collected there like mustard gas settling into a trench. An Endless Chatter of Monotony murmured and echoed off veneer walls covered in tacky home-style décor, deer-head wall mounts, cuckoo clocks, and various other worthless collections of bric-a-brac. Beside a old treadle sewing machine, a newly patched pair of torn green sweatpants lay folded with care. With their losses mounting under the Service Industry's land charge, the Biddies had ensconced themselves in their bricolage abode and had administered triage where necessary. Their counterplot was well under way.

"It's only a matter of time," stank the Head Biddy.

The Biddies, after collecting a sufficient amount of deer scent glands from their unruly deer-processing sons, had cooked the majority of the glands down in non-reactionary stock pots into a thick, foul soup.

"Thicker, thicker," stewed the Sous-Biddy of Nasal Operations.

She threw in some turnips.

The rest of the scent glands were painstakingly milked of their fatty oils by quavering, arthritic Biddy-fingers. Pheromones dripped. Pustules popped. In place of white laboratory coats, well-stained kitchen aprons hung from old Biddy necks. Numerous local herbs and weeds were distilled and added to the cooled broth. Only the Head Biddy and three of her trusted Noses knew the recipe. The Long Vines of Endless Gossip remained mum on the Biddies' secret formula. The curiosity of Science was therefore aroused.

"*Lindera benzoin*—spicebush, for sure," sniffed one of our high school science teachers. "And probably yarrow. We'll have to run some tests."

The Biddies mixed and refined their new essence in a pure bath of Biddy moonshine, glycerin, and distilled Tainted Creek water. They aged the product for six weeks in glass mayonnaise jars.

"These jars need boiled again," stank the Head Biddy. "I can still smell dilly beans and sauerkraut."

Now, the fragrance was done. The bouquet had blossomed, the molecules had married, the purr was ready to fume.

Months after the Biddies initial implementation of Project Auld, a plan conceived like a stink bomb, row after row of blue-gray-headed Biddies worked from sunup to sundown stuffing packets with their new Aroma-Weapon: Odeur Nouveau. No effort had so aligned the various factions within the Brigade since their last Stitch-n-Bitch meeting, which, notably, had produced a queen-sized Amish quilt for charity in less than four hours. Even the weekly bingo games at Our Sacred Virgin on the Hill Church paled in comparison to the great melding of ancient wills then congregated inside the Ole Homestead.

EARPLUGS

"Stuff 'em and pack 'em! Stuff 'em and pack 'em! That's it!" yelled baton-wielding Biddy Bulls, as they paced behind countless rows of gray, bobbing Biddy heads.

Rhubarb pie tins and Crock-Pots of ham and beans set to:

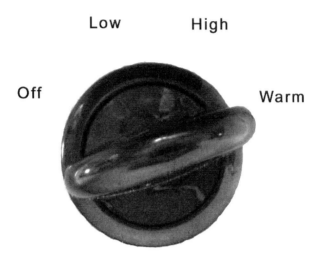

Low   High

Off   Warm

sat about the cloistral rooms untouched. A complex mixture of Old and New wafted in and out and over and between the hand-hewn old barn rafters that held the Ole Homestead aright. Eau de Auld and Odeur Nouveau had become mythological black snakes twined in an unholy coitus caduceus. The smell was immense, overwhelming, and more than a bit like a pop song.

"Through their nostrils we will come."

They worked with diligence.

"Through their noses they will follow."

It would not be long.

THE FAIRGROUNDS

One night I walked to our fairgrounds. I would go to the Fairgrounds sometimes when it was dark, and our town had laid down its head for the night. Like the railroad and the horse, most of the fairgrounds in our region had been relegated to the past and largely abandoned. History had passed them by in lieu of movie theaters, video games, television programs, and motor vehicles.

"Vehicles enable us to travel faster and farther," preached My Only Friend in Town, "while encouraging our destinations and our dreams into the Ever Beyond. It's a paradox. The closer cars take us, the farther we want and need to go."

Motors were good for Tourism; they were not so good for downtown. My Only Friend in Town said that someday the car would meet its fate and become a relic like the Fairgrounds. Perhaps he was right, and the horse would ride again. But for now, our town's collective fascination with the horse, as a mode of transport for either work or entertainment, had long ended. Instead of breeding horses to race at the local fair, we built hot-rods and customized our trucks with mud-running monster tires and supercharged engines, or rode four-wheelers, or dirt bikes. We burned fuel and shredded earth and rode the mechanical beast. Occasionally, a jockey would still harness up a horse and a racing buggy and gallop around the Fairgrounds' track like an anachronism, but mostly these things had had their day, like our town before Tourism.

I once had a conversation with the Only Other Customer in Town about horses. I was walking through town and saw a stream of foamy bubbles running down the gutter. The Only Other Customer in Town stood in his driveway giving his car a loving bath.

"I've got a bunch of horses," shammied the Only Other Customer in Town, as he polished his muscle car. "Four hundred and fifty of 'em! Under my hood!"

To reach the Fairgrounds on the eastern edge of town, I traversed a series of our brick sidewalks. The bricks were like a moving documentary of plate tectonics at work. Falls occurred here. Blood was spilled. Scraped knees and stubbed toes competed for injurious honors. The best thing to do was to keep your head down and to not look up too much, a feat that I had nearly perfected at an early age by making a game of walking on the bricks in precise patterns while trying not to think too much about the town and about the volume all around me.

The sidewalks in town were once smooth and maintained. Every four years or so after the Brick Factory supplied the pavers, city maintenance crews, local business sponsors, or prospective

Eagle Scouts would pull up the bricks and re-lay them in a nice bed of sandstone-pulverized sand. Now, no one cared. There was no money for such endeavors, and no time for it either. Sidewalks in many parts of town had long since been converted to concrete, just as the brick kilns had been replaced by the reservoirs of the Concrete Company. The Concrete Company dug sand and siphoned water up and down the Meandering River floodplain. When the sand gave out, the gouged-out reservoirs became man-made lakes for tourists and fishermen, eyesores of Commerce beside the pock-marked river. But there were still plenty of neglected brick sidewalks in town, especially in the residential neighborhoods close to downtown.

"Oh, look at all the geese!" said a carload of tourists, as they sped past a working concrete operation.

Across the railroad tracks and in front of dilapidated houses, I stumbled over the fault lines of our tectonic brick sidewalks, onward toward the Fairgrounds' gate.

Around the perimeter fence of the Fairgrounds, ancient shade trees grew like wardens. Oak, ash, broken box elder, and silver maple trees loomed as they had for decades down on the carnivals, the horse races, the demolition derby events, and the murky shadows of outlying grange buildings. Many a virgin had the trees seen deflowered, and many a night had they looked away.

I passed the trees.

EARPLUGS

Lisa.

Inside the Fairgrounds, multiple outbuildings had been erected over the years by civically upstanding Lions Clubs and other cults within our town: stages, horse barns, pavilions, cattle pens, refreshment stands, klieg lights. I headed straight for the Grandstand, but did not know why. The Grandstand: a place I seldom visited, yet one that held so much history and so many collective memories for our town. As I ascended the Grandstand's worn sandstone steps, I thought of a time when things were more innocent, and fireworks would explode in the festive Fourth of July sky over our town's gleaming, happy, and upturned faces. Shells would fire from the infield track in one combination of three colors and designs: red, silver, or blue; round, sparkly, or dud. From the Grandstand's splintered wooden bleachers, we would sit and witness the spectacle, while out on the infield town firefighters like ninjas darted here and there from fuse to fuse, igniting rockets that would shoot up and up, like victory, into the cool dark summer sky.

Now, the Fairgrounds hosted but three annual events: our town's aforementioned Fourth of July Jamboree and Fireworks Display, which was down to two colors of shells and rumored to be burning the last of its long-storied fuse; the Ugly Carnival, which clung to life as if it were the last wispy strand of cotton candy in an otherwise empty plastic bag; and the Fair, which was thinking about changing its name to the Derby. It was all run-down, ironically, except for the Derby. Horses still ran the Fairgrounds' track sometimes—listless loops of sulking sulkies—but the Derby had been co-opted like a Christian holiday built on pagan beliefs. The Fair brought the Derby, and everybody liked the Derby. Everyone loved the loud Demolition Derby.

My earplugs were like communism in our town.

From the Grandstand, I stood and looked out at the lonesome track and the abandoned infield. The stars shone down and the hills rose up like dark turtle shells on the horizon, and I began to cry.

So much had been lost, and I could not hear a thing.

THE SPOT

There was a spot outside our town that young couples or good friends would sometimes go to: the Spot. Located twelve miles from town off a state highway, the Spot was really just a dirt-topped knoll. The knoll offered a fantastic view of some of our particularly picturesque rolling hills. The Service Industry often cited such vistas as the Spot in her speeches on Tourism to regional business leaders or to investment bankers. She said, "You wouldn't believe some of our rolling hills—rolling in money!"

The Spot was also a lonely place, which was peculiar because no one ever went to the Spot alone. The Spot was a social place like rum and coke and always traveled in pairs.

"We should bring them out here the next time we come," said a girl.

"Yeah," said a nervous boy, "that might be cool."

"NO," said the Spot and instead offered them a panoramic view of the night stars.

The boy and the girl stood at the Spot and thought about their lives, and about the depth of the night sky, and about the place they stood now, wrapped in a planetarium blanket.

"It's beautiful," cooed the girl.

"You're beautiful," said the boy.

The Spot worked like this. It also worked for having a cigarette with a good friend, if you could count on good friends.

In the coming months, a time in which My Only Friend in Town would die, the Service Industry would transform the Spot into an official Scenic Overlook with a paved pull-over parking area and one gray coin-operated viewing machine.

signs would hang on guardrails above the mounting garbage. Vehicles left after dark were subject to immediate investigation for Boredom Relief.

The view was just as beautiful, but the Spot would become somehow changed. From that point on, the Spot refused to communicate anything but its sweeping fields of binary pleasure.

And the Spot, being a lonely place, would become lonelier still.

THE TEN-CENT DINER

"Oh . . . hello," said the Service Industry.

I was downtown drinking black coffee at the Ten Cent Diner, where the coffee cost sixty-two cents and the apple pie was good. The tabletop before me was filled with air where sugar packets, empty white plastic non-dairy creamer containers, cigarette packages, nickels, lighters, and friends should have been.

I sat and stared at the laminate oak finish of the diner table and drank coffee all night and thought about the town, and about Lisa, and about My Only Friend in Town, and about the forces that tear our lives apart. The Service Industry had come in for a late night snack of French-fried potatoes and ketchup after a hard long day in her office across the street. At her desk in the Mayor's Office, the Service Industry had spent the entire day scrupulously devising ways to appropriately entitle her new plans, which were really just old plans like wolves in wolf clothing.

My cup of coffee surfed over the undulating grain of the oak tabletop in search of the perfect wave.

"Can I sit here?" the Service Industry asked, always ready to woo a potential vote. Before me, she placed an expensive designer purse onto the cheap pressed-wood of the tabletop. Her purse was decorated with a single letter over and over again as if the letter were a stuttering logo perpetually stuck on the first consonant of its own name. As the Service Industry talked, her lips moved and swayed like the ghosts of trees sacrificed on the busy altar of Growth.

"Are you wearing earplugs?" the Service Industry queried and delicately moved to a table opposite mine. After situating her purse away from a few globs of mustard and the partially solidified remains of a country-fried steak, the Service Industry summoned the lazy waitress.

"French fries and a milk, please. Thanks, hon."

The lazy waitress looked at her and shuffled away, a grease-coated pellicle of the American Dream.

On the tabletop, my coffee cup caught an amber wave of grain and rode it for all that it was worth.

The Service Industry glanced at the cup and turned her attention back to me.

Full of tact and the sure ability to connect with any county denizen, she screamed, "SO, WHAT'S UP WITH THE EARPLUGS?"

In the back kitchen, her French fries popped and sputtered into crispy fact.

"The town is very small," I replied. "And I'd prefer not to hear

EARPLUGS

it."

Sensing movement, the Service Industry waved off an impending coffee attack before it had even occurred to the lazy waitress to grab the coffee pot.

"SO, YOU'RE TRYING TO SHUT US OUT?" the Service Industry loudly dictated.

I stared at my chipped coffee mug and the empty tabletop before me. I imagined the Service Industry at home in front of a large oval mirror practicing the Endless Chatter of Monotony over and over to herself without ever quite grasping the point.

I said, "Maybe I'm trying to shut everything in."

The lazy waitress lit a cigarette in a corner booth and thought of life beyond work.

"THAT DOESN'T MAKE SENSE," cried the Service Industry, in a raspy voice like verbal exhaustion.

The Only Other Customer in Town materialized at a side table and said, "Baked beans."

As the Service Industry's gaze shifted, machinations on Tourism quickly set to work deep inside her skull.

I slid sixty-two gooey cents and a half dollar tip into the tide of the tabletop and stood up to leave. As the chimes over the glass door tinkled a muted good-bye, I barely heard the beginnings of a new Evil Plan.

Inside the Ten Cent Diner, the Service Industry sat leaning

forward in a booth with the Only Other Customer in Town. Together they outlined a precise seven-step plan for christening an inaugural town nickname: Baked Bean City.

Like a redesigned American eagle on the Great Seal of the United States, the Service Industry gripped her logoed purse in one hand and a greasy French fry between two fingers in the other. As she bit into the fry, the steaming tuber smoked as if it were an idling backhoe ready to break ground on a frost-laden winter morning.

"Finally, our town would step into the Modern World of Tourism and adopt a bona fide, attention-grabbing, historically inaccurate, and completely frivolous moniker!" cheered the Service Industry, like a pompom shaking at half-time.

At Leo's, the boxes of Boston Baked Beans wept.

"Maybe we could utilize the old Brick Factory somehow. Make it a Bean Factory."

Far out in nature's scenic wonderland, our sun-dappled hills; breath-taking caves; stately forests; healthy, if somewhat overpopulated, wildlife; depleted natural resources; and empty coal seams issued a great collective sigh of "Fuck!"

"We got screwed," complained a wood duck.

"Again," lamented a disregarded chunk of bituminous coal.

Red second-place ribbons and purple participation-only ribbons were metaphorically handed out and quickly stuffed in unused

EARPLUGS

burrows, in hollowed-out logs, in still-smoldering abandoned mine-shafts, and in the underwear drawer of the ruffed grouse.

Back at the diner, the Only Other Customer in Town spilled the beans and said, "The whole secret is a little more mustard."

Meanwhile, the Service Industry rapidly finalized the rough draft of her Baked Bean Plan, which went something like this: Steps One through Five mentioned Tourism and Steps Six and Seven mentioned the Only Other Customer in Town re-opening, possibly on the old Brick Factory grounds, his hitherto failed bean shop. In accordance with Step Seven, the Only Other Customer in Town would also serve as chairman of the soon-to-be chartered Baked Bean Festival Committee, which would meet weekly from that point forward, ad infinitum, for French fries and milk at the Ten Cent Diner.

Coffee was optional; ketchup was extra.

"Make sure they're not half-baked," warned the Only Other Customer in Town. "The beans."

Despite the occasional lapse in bean-honored local leadership, the Ten Cent Diner would need a second waitress.

Our local economy surged.

The Service Industry had done it again.

The Ten Cent Diner changed hands the next week. The new owners from Somewhere Else renamed it the Sandstone Cliffs with Pretty Hills and Classy Food Restaurant. They hired a chef, fired the lazy waitress, replaced her with high school kids from the west side of town, designated Friday night as Baked Bean Friday, and had live music imported from the state capital three nights a week.

Tourists poured in and spent a fortune.

The price of a cup of coffee rose well above sixty-two cents, but the apple pie remained unfailingly good.

Baked Bean City.

O, I wish I had never heard it.

Weeks from death, My Only Friend in Town said, "Dude, I wonder if I could get a show there? They might hire me, and it'd be pretty cool."

I pushed hard on my earplugs.

GETTING NASTY

Things invariably resorted to getting nasty in our town.

For instance, in the next chapter, I am unaware of the car that hits me after I stumble backward and fall off one of our concrete sidewalks into the main intersection of downtown Main Street. The selfsame intersection where the small, sad trailer of Santa Clause parked year in and year out around Christmastime to snap hopeless photos of our town's children while listening to their wistful catalogue dreams. As the car strikes me, I am hurled through the air like a peppermint candy cane thrown from a Christmas parade float, all broken red and white.

"My back hurts," I say, as I writhe around in the street in front of the Kountry Kupboards Bulk Foods Store.

"Looks bad, son. Call the corpsman," says an old farmer. The old farmer was a veteran of World War II. He wore a U.S. Navy ball cap with gold embroidered lettering, an embossed ship, and plenty of emblematic hat pins. The old vet's farm had been foreclosed on three years before. He had nothing better to do now than to walk about town grumbling and wearing his hat.

A local developer, spurred on by the Service Industry and

backed by her close friend, the Banking Industry, had purchased the old farmer's land for a pittance.

The old farmer's erstwhile farm now sported fifteen new rental cabins and the Family Fun for All Center. The Family Fun for All Center stood in what was once the old vet's prime rotational corn and soybean field, grazing for money. The field was very large: fifty acres. His family had called it the Family Food for All Field. The Family Food for All Field in its current state consisted of: the rental cabins, tourists, a miniature golf course with plastic greens like the hook side of Velcro, a gift shop called the Gift Shoppe, four refreshment stands, a bunch of crappy rides, more plastic, trash, and a pen of cooped-up, sickly-looking albino deer. The deer could be hand fed through a chain link fence for an American quarter. The deer's food, corn, was kept in red supermarket-exit gumball vending machines located right beside the chain link fence. The machines would not accept Canadian coin. A Canadian quarter would simply disappear into the pay box, never to deliver one altruistic kernel of goodwill. Only American currency would do for these deer. Kind-hearted tourists would put their American quarter into one of the vending machines, twist the heavy metal dial, and out would come a handful of No. 2 field corn like so many unsanitary M&M's, or a bouncy rubber ball, or a stale collection of unsalted peanuts. Ironically, both the deer and the corn were shipped in from Somewhere Else. The deer did not seem to mind the corn, but they did look sickly.

"Mommy, I want to feed the deer!"

"Ok, sweetie. Watch your fingers."

"Corn," ruminated a bored white doe. "Corn."

But for now, before the accident in the next chapter with the car, while I was still able to walk and to talk and to hear very little, things in town had just begun to get nasty. The young women in town all wore that smell, and it was maddening: Odeur Nouveau. Lust and hatred co-mingled in a death match of conspiracy. Men salivated. Women swaggered. Pheromones and acne burst forth in resplendent displays of affection rivalling the manic drumming display of the male ruffed grouse, or the strutting dance of a hormone-crazed wild turkey, or the mewing weirdness of a house cat ready for action.

I headed for the Old Iron Trestle and thought of times past. My, I was young. My earplugs felt like the weight of a hundred years.

Down at the Trestle, I met My Only Friend in Town and he said, "The doomsayers are fools, but the righteous will not prevail."

The pink headband was gone from the wet rock.

I kicked a broken railroad spike and a few chunks of limestone down through the creosoted ties and into the Meandering River. They fell heavily down and each landed with a *kerplunk*. The river would not carry them Away.

The Biddy Brigade had spread their will.

And Lisa stunk with them.

LISA

I saw her as I rounded the corner by the Hardware Store onto Main Street and read the:

> ## STOP IN FOR THE SMELL!

sign for the thousandth time.

Lisa stood across the street with her back to me like the polar opposite of magnetic force. She wore a pink coat and a green sash with yellow sneakers, and I ran across the street to her like a rerun. As I closed within yards, Lisa turned to me, and the stench of the Biddies' new beauty butter hit me and hit me hard. I coughed. I gagged. I wondered if my hair would fall out. I was knocked back several feet and stumbled off the curb.

"AHHH!" I yelled.

I fell backward into Main Street. Eau de Auld and Odeur Nouveau swirled about me in a sinister mushroom-clouded vapor. A pristinely-kept Buick Century driven by a treacherous old Biddy on her way to the C.F.G. to buy some dry beans and oatmeal struck me as I fell into her path. I flew across the road, injured. My earplugs flew from my ears and landed on Main Street like spent bullet casings from shots that missed.

"It's so wonderful to hear," I sighed, in shock and impending pain.

I lay there broken on the street and listened to the bustle of Commerce. I heard motor engines gunning through red stop lights. I heard pigeons cooing from long unused second-story windows. I heard footsteps and the murmurings of townsfolk as they gathered about my body. The old farmer grumbled in his hat. I heard Lisa scream, "But darling, it's only Odeur Nouveau!" as if she were playing the part of a wronged heroine in an old black-and-white movie, or perhaps a campy bimbo in a TV infomercial. I heard angels and devils and great cosmic sounds like the end of the American Dream. A butterfly flew above my eyes and was smashed by the arriving ambulance. O, chaos be damned. I heard the far off sound of the Meandering River, as it escaped from our town.

And I listened and listened, but I could not hear the end, as the river filtered quietly Away.

ANOMALY CASTLE AND THE ORDER OF THE FORGOTTEN

I came to in the Only Hospital Around, our local hospital on the northeast side of town. The Only Hospital Around served three counties and lay on a forgotten road. People in town forgot about the road until they drove out that way to see the hospital, and then they remembered that the Only Hospital Around was there on the Forgotten Road.

"Let's take this road today," a couple might decide on a Sunday drive through the county.

"Sure, I forgot this road was here."

"Hey, there's the hospital," one of the townspersons will exclaim.

"I thought it was around here somewhere," the other townsperson will reply. "I always forget that it's here, even though it seems like the only one around."

If the townspeople were young, they usually said these things while driving monster-tired trucks or old, used, run-down cars fit only for the young or for the severely dispossessed. But if the townspeople were old, they often said these things on Sunday drives through the countryside in cars mounted with plates marked:

It made them feel good to drive the old cars. The heavy steel frames and the oversize steering wheels were something to hold on to, like savings bonds on Sunday. The townspeople had long ago traded in their horses, yet they would not so easily part with their vintage cars. They would trot these cars out when the weather was fine, and the trees were pretty, and the air of nostalgia would wash over the clean polished steel of yesteryear. The townspeople would believe then that things were somehow once better, or someway more simple. They would smile and toot their rooty-tooty horns and admire the fine autumn trees. They would feel then as if their lives were good, and once again worth living, and that all that had passed was true and was the way that life should be.

"We'd better get some gas," an old townsperson driving a 1956 two-tone Plymouth Belvedere might say. "And probably a new V-belt."

The old townsperson pushes in the transmission. The historical vehicle races past the Only Hospital Around and on down the Forgotten Road.

The Only Hospital Around was staffed by two very quiet doctors and ten nurses that all lived together in a castle. One of the doctors was so quiet that we will never hear from him. He will remain silent throughout this story as if he were an invisible Marcel Marceau or a forgotten prisoner locked away in the dungeon of a castle—chained, possibly bleeding, but formless and unimportant—his white doctor's tunic but a ghost-like sheet in the dark night of undeveloped character.

He will not.

Be able to help.

The castle in which the nurses and the two doctors lived was called Anomaly Castle. People in town had named the castle because, well, it was a castle. The castle sat on a hill overlooking the emergency ward on the backside of the hospital. It was the only castle in town. Some folks in town had wanted to name the castle the Only Castle in Town, but a vote was taken and Anomaly Castle won by a vote of 1,202 to 857. It was a rare victory for vocabulary. The castle was gray and had one turret and it was shrouded in trees like a leafy moat and was quite mysterious.

I awoke in a white room in the hospital, and my head hurt.

"Where am I?" I wondered out loud, catching a whiff of something familiar and unpleasant.

"You're in the Only Hospital Around," decreed a nurse-princess, exuding Odeur Nouveau like a brand new copy of

Cosmopolitan magazine. The magazine was turned to the page of a perfume advertisement. On the page of the perfume advertisement, a perfume sample opened under a flap of the page. The flap folded back to reveal a sticky glue and the perfume smell, and the nurse-princess was smiling. She said, "I came down from the castle when I heard the sirens."

I grabbed a pair of calipers and a few primitive charts of the sun, the moon, and the stars—common items on the Forgotten Road—and began calculations that might equate to a possible route home from an unknown, emergency-staffed location. O, astrolabe in hand! O, wide sea in my eyes! Scenes from the Salsa Vendor's unexplainable voyages flashed through my mind: unavoidable sirens, mermaids with long blonde hair, sea serpents like hypodermic needles, nine pound catheters, death ships and typhoons, a dead calm against the *beep beep beeping* of a sea gull heart rate machine. I twitched my fingers to escape the nightmare; my mouth tasted of brine.

I wadded up a few pieces of napkin from the tray beside my bed and stuffed them into my ears.

"That seems like good science, but really you should use your innate tracking skills like Tom Brown does in all of those books of his," critiqued My Only Friend in Town, scaring the napkins out of my ears from the corner of the white room. "Or maybe, once you're in the sun, try the Shadowless Stick Method to find a rough east/west direction from which you can orient yourself," he advised.

The calipers fell from my hand and clinked across the white-tiled floor. A primitive chart of Gemini rerolled itself by the E.K.G. machine.

"What are you doing here? What happened?"

"I followed you out here on the Forgotten Road," said My Only Friend in Town.

"I didn't think you were downtown."

"I had plenty of time to get ready," rehearsed My Only Friend in Town. "It's like at a show when the band is supposed to start at ten, but really always starts a lot later."

"Oh," I said. "Lisa?"

"I also heard the news through the Long Vines of Endless Gossip, so I ran downtown to follow the ambulance," panted My Only Friend in Town. "The ambulance had left already, but they had to drive around town four or five times because they forgot which road the hospital was on. Luckily, they finally decided to take the Forgotten Road, because I was getting pretty tired from yelling obscenities, and from running after them, and of course from just trying to keep my bearings."

As if he were an unannounced angel, Pastor Thirty-Seven walked abruptly into the room and intoned, "I hope you're feeling better, son. Our prayers are with you," and left.

Awestruck, My Only Friend in Town cried, "Dude, I can't believe all thirty-seven of our priests and ministers have been in here to see you already. When I was out on the road, nobody believed in God."

I said, "I forget where we are."

"Sure," ordained My Only Friend in Town. "It's arbitrary, like running laps at the community gym."

My doctor, Doctor Obvious, rode in then and proclaimed, "Your wearing earplugs is symptomatic of keeping the town at bay," and galloped off like sunlight glistening on chainmail.

I felt as confused and as introspective as usual when talking with people from our town. My head pulsed. A sound like the void of small-town claustrophobia drew to a crescendo in my naked, earplug-less ears. My Only Friend in Town stood over my bed, strangely quiet.

I needed earplugs.

Perhaps I could just drift off to whatever pharmaceutical wonderland petered down from the I.V. dangling above me.

Drip.

Drip.

Shit.

Saline.

The crescendo rose and rose and soon enveloped me in a shock-induced nightmare of slumber. I shook. I sweated. My head banged and hurt.

And I dreamed.

In my dream, I was out on the Meandering River in a canoe, all alone, and the river swept on—heedless of my J-Stroke perfection. I realized that I was paddling upstream and that clouds had begun to come in like perfume bottles on my perfect day. I paddled and paddled going Nowhere, unable to turn, and my arms began to tire. I continued to paddle, but the river held me, and our town was all around. At last, exhausted, I laid the oar down and lifted my face to a dying black sun. The black dying sun was like a burnt baked bean in the sky, and the clouds circled about it like a halo. Then the river stopped. Calm at last.

I was never leaving.

My Only Friend in Town shook me then, hard on the shoulder, and his face was a wrinkle. I awoke to the other familiar stench: Eau de Auld. Biddy perfume filled the sterile halls of the Only Hospital Around like the overripe smell of a bloated floral corpse. It was as if the Biddies had awoken that day to find a dead bouquet of two-week old flowers wilted upon their kitchen table. Partial to the smell, the Biddies decided to douse themselves with the ripe standing water inside the vase. On top of the vase water, the Biddies added a potent chemical cocktail and a few extra drops of *essence of cadaver*. It was an unwelcome smell. Doom was imminent. Around us, pristine white walls cowered against themselves. Used syringes wept. Soiled bedpans begged for reprieve. Latex surgeon's gloves felt helpless to help. The reigning king of putridity, Hospital Food, shrank in fear.

"Succumb to the permeating pressure of Biddy plenitude!" preached Pastor Three from somewhere down the hall.

And I realized, as if we were all prescription bottles in a tightly cramped medicine cabinet, that Biddies were everywhere: Biddy-kids and -grandkids filled the emergency waiting room; crotchety old Biddy-women wandered the short-term care ward; silent Biddy-men lined the long-term bed rows; Biddy-babies suckled in the birthing center; and Biddy Brigade Welcome Committee members, with arms full of peanut butter cookies, roamed the halls in search of . . . someone, anyone, there had to be Another. Odeur Nouveau, which had filled my room since the arrival of the nurse-princess, and which had hitherto been content to find purchase where possible in the sterile environs of the sanitary, now groveled like a thin, pretty model of subordination, hiding beneath fashion magazines and gossip rags on the bedside tables of the impotent and the infirm.

O, Stench of the Ages, turn me not into stone!

In his most honest and indie way, My Only Friend in Town sang, "Dude, this reminds me of this time I was taking a leak in this dive bar up in Cleveland. It reeks. Let's get out of here."

I picked up my napkin-plugs from the floor.

"OK," I said.

We stumbled away to find our town.

EARPLUGS

SWOOSH

There was a time when I walked through our town like a shadow boxer. Jabs left and jabs right. Swinging to miss really. I would stand in position and hate at the thought.

"Swoosh," said the air.

"Huh, huh," I would swing.

Our town would usually ignore my blows. It had enough on its plate. It could hear the bells of change like a digital alarm clock at 3AM on a cold winter morning. Our town was surrounded by comforting blankets and the nice aroma of percolating Folgers on the kitchen stove; it did not want to get out of bed.

But all that was gone. We all knew.

"Swoosh, swoosh." My balled fists swept through the air like pistons, and the air parted around them like sighs.

A FOOL'S COURSE

After finding our way home to the west side from the hospital and resting up for a few days, My Only Friend in Town and I decided to go out on the Meandering River and pretend that we were sailing Away for the very last time.

I thought of my dream.

"It's a fool's course," said My Only Friend in Town. "Nothing turns out the way it's supposed to, yet you still keep doing it even though you know it won't work out."

My head had healed a bit. A new pair of earplugs sat in my ears like a mother's lunch on a rainy afternoon.

My Only Friend in Town said, "I always preferred tomato soup and grilled cheese. She cut my grilled cheese sandwiches diagonally, and they tasted better that way."

We had rented a canoe at the Meandering River Livery and were passing families with scared toddlers and drunken university students at a fairly good pace. The smell of tobacco wafted back to us from some cigarette-smoking locals up ahead and had sparked numerous and luminous ruminations from My Only Friend in Town. It was as if he were back on the road.

"The turtles hide from us because they're scared," said My

Only Friend in Town.

"Fuck you!" burbled a sleek softshell turtle, as it sank to hoary depths.

A multitude of dragonflies hovered nearby, moot on the subject, but with knowing looks.

"Sometimes I just need to seek redemption."

I took my earplugs out of my ears and jumped overboard, tired of it. Under the water, the channel swept about me as if it were a painted argument between Mystery and Suspense. The water was close. "This one time I was in Texas and liked it," remembered My Only Friend in Town. "We played this bar and nobody gave a shit."

He talked to no one in particular. Perhaps the dragonflies listened. I moved through the water, and my sneakers became heavy.

My Only Friend in Town said, "I thought it was fun anyway." He began to run in place on the drifting, it-used-to-be-fun canoe.

I resurfaced, lay back in the current, and watched the sky with my ears safely below the waterline.

"SWIM!" yelled a school of spotted bass. "THEY'RE RIGHT THERE!"

On the river, I bathed.

As the current moved against my legs, I felt the sweep and the pull of the eternal. My sneakers clung to my feet like irons. I remembered a time when I drove past our town's dam. The dam held back our town's man-made lake: Town Lake. At one time, before the trees grew back and the Service Industry came along, Town Lake was the only real blip on our tourist radar. The lake was built in the bygone days of the Works Progress Administration (W.P.A.), when Big Government stepped in to save its drowning little brother, Almost as Big Government. The W.P.A. gave folks something to do—build lakes, build schools, build roads—while Big Government tried to figure out how to re-roll the life preserver ropes and re-hang that cumbersome life hook called America.

In addition to Town Lake proper, the W.P.A. also created the Small and Sandy Town Lake Beach, the Back of the Lake, fishing, pontoon boating, and lots of mosquitoes. Like hands in a classroom, vacation homes went up around the easy-answer lake. The recently relocated Clay Pipe Products and Manufacturing Company sold record amounts of clay sewer pipe during those halcyon fiscal quarters of Growth. Shaped remarkably enough like a toilet bowl, Town Lake also moonlighted as a septic tank for countless homes outfitted with Clay Pipe's nearly indestructible clay sewer pipe. Like cloacae, the clay pipes vented their collective goods into the turbid waters, and the catfish, the common carp, and the fisherman thrived. Not to be outdone in fouling the stream, squadrons of Canada Geese from Somewhere Else heard of the potential new layover through the Long Vines of Endless Gossip and eyed the new stop like tourists from afar. The geese pulled out their planning journals, maps, passports, and G.O.R.P. and set a long-eyed thirty-year course of recovery, debarkation, and takeover. Upon landing, around the same time that the Service Industry first came to power, the geese immediately pooped all over the place.

"Honk, honk," said a goose.

Another creek drowned; another field lost: Tourism.

Up in the canoe, My Only Friend in Town thoughtfully picked his nose and said, "I think picking your nose is underrated as a form of meditation."

After driving past the dam of my memories, I arrived home that night to find a very short poem about the town and about the dam in a one-off Poetry Corner feature of the *Local Daily*, our town newspaper. The author was listed as Walt Ginsberg, and I suspected that My Only Friend in Town was behind it. I remembered that poem now as I swam under the Meandering River and as my memory-self drove by the lake on the highway where My Only Friend in Town would soon wreck his four-door sedan and die coming home from a party.

The poem was sad as such poems should be and was titled "A Sixty-Two Cent Meal."

It went like this:

THE POETRY CORNER

A Sixty-Two Cent Meal
by Walt Ginsberg

A solitary night
in a crash-and-dive coffee joint
nestled away in a lost boom town
trying to gain a second breath
in its hills
and rocks
with suburban onlookers cam-cording waterfalls
or dams that leak a small stream of water
from a Depression-era lake
where a tree limb sometimes teeters on its edge
and becomes an instant success
for faraway television nights of wine
and cheese
while here it is only coffee
and water
a sixty-two cent meal
amid country gossip
and an underpaid waitress.

I came out of the water and climbed into the canoe.

"Damn, I love picking my nose," said My Only Friend in Town.

"I can breathe so much better."

EARPLUGS

THE SECRET

I should have known that it was over when Lisa told me her secret.

The secret was like a small child's tooth. Lisa had kept the small white tooth in a doe-skin medicine bag, which hung about her neck, and between her breasts and her long blonde hair, and down beside her heart. The medicine bag was pretty, but what lay inside was rotten and white.

Eventually, Lisa emptied the bag, and the small white tooth toppled out. It sat before us as if it were a smoldering beacon, or an unhygienic lighthouse, and our relationship sailed on.

"That's not an eyetooth," I said. "It's a lie-tooth."

Out on the seas of love, Lisa and I watched from a slippery deck and marveled at the sweeping light from the small white tooth, as the winds whirled and a fog as thick as toothpaste wrapped about our bodies.

"Watch out for the rocks!" Lisa yelled, as we made out for the last time.

"Dammit," I said. "It was so nice at first."

Saliva and sleet sheered down at ruthless angles and beat upon our lovesick shores.

My bloated canvas sneakers sloshed back and forth across the deck of our flimsy relationship. Looking out on the horizon, I could just make out the soft rolling hills of our town and of our county, which were almost upon me again. The smell of the sea was replaced by Eau de Auld. The air felt like time. The taste of the saltwater on Lisa's lips was the primordial stew of Odeur Nouveau. Tiny flecks of sand and of grit ground into the soles of my feet, and between my toes, and also inside my ears. But I was not on the river, and there would be no pearl.

There would be earplugs.

"Six sheets to the wind and nine points to the north!" ballyhooed My Only Friend in Town, bursting from a stowaway closet.

My Only Friend in Town climbed the mast to the crow's nest of our relationship and sang, "I met this girl on the road once. She worked at a dentist's office and had a plaque scraper like a miniature pirate hook. It didn't work out, although I still think about her sometimes when I'm brushing my teeth."

We hit the rocks.

"I hate those things," said My Only Friend in Town.

For the white tooth was not as it seemed, as small white children's teeth are wont to be. Impermanent things never are. Small white children's teeth cannot hold back time, or grief, or the inevitable fury of betrayal and of change. Older and wiser teeth wait in an upstairs cabin like impatient victims of a coming storm,

EARPLUGS

like bridesmaids before a doomed wedding party, like dentists with too large fingers.

But that tooth.

The tooth was hard to extract. It was slippery; it was crafty; it was difficult to pull out. That tooth had been in there for a while and sort of liked it. But once released, the warm salty seas of blood washed over us, and our relationship foundered and sunk on the shallow, temporal shoals of Young Love.

Perhaps if Lisa had mentioned the secret after twenty-three minutes, perhaps as a loving band-aid were placed upon her knee, or as another lame movie ended in a snuggling tryst of post-copulation, things would have been OK, but after 23,861 minutes and forty-three seconds, her not telling was a harbinger of things to come.

Like a cavity, the secret would consume us from within. There was no filling; there was no turning back.

Her words cut through the air and into my ears like loud broken plate-glass cannonballs, and I did not want to hear it.

Anymore.

And Lisa left.

Our town roared back in.

FREE BEER AND THE ERA OF THE BYGONE

My Only Friend in Town said, "Confirmation of the mystery has been communicated."

I did not know what he meant as usual, but his cryptic notion gave me some certain sense of hope, like a koan that had an answer.

"I can say for sure that I'm going to go through with it," devised My Only Friend in Town. "Like that time we were stranded in our van after the transmission went out on our way to the show, and we decided to haul our gear the last seven miles on foot to try to make the gig."

I hurriedly thumbed through my worn, stolen 1959 copy of *Zen Buddhism*.

Flip. Flip. "Did you make it?" I asked.

"No," said My Only Friend in Town, "but we got free beer."

I left My Only Friend in Town in his trim little red and white shack and began walking toward the center of town. Across the mud-filled streets of the west side, across the Old Iron Trestle, over the Meandering River, where the pink headband once rested silently on a smooth, wet rock, and then through our town streets and on into downtown.

The bakery had closed its aromatic doors.

The flowers at the Flower Shop had turned capitulation white.

Odeur Nouveau reigned.

There were times now when our town was Far Away. I could not hear the creaking moan of its weight like bell towers intoning the time. I walked our town's brick-lined streets, and suddenly the town exploded like an enormous glockenspiel cuckoo clock on the hour, but without so much of the sound. Birds spun and twiddled. Old farmers like wooden figurines in blue overalls danced down Main Street. The smell of decay and of passing time permeated the air. Old-time. Past time. O, earplugs. The era of the bygone. Walking the streets that were once boardwalks and new. Weather and fire and real estate. The changing of the guard, the old versus the new, the sound and the muffled fury.

The Service Industry, drenched in Odeur Nouveau, bustled past me on the sidewalk, late for a sit-down Ecotourism meeting on Place and the Cultural Environment of Nowhere.

I thought of that pink headband and of hard rocks and of the twining corkscrew flow of water down the long Meandering River — silt and sandstone, memories and love, dreams and time — all etched and flushed away like crumbling tombstones and forgotten old names.

Stumbling on, I passed a group of adolescent local bullies sitting in the back of a mud-splattered, monster-tired pick-up truck parked on Main Street.

"Hey, aren't you that freak that wears those earplugs?" they yelled. Their eyes followed me like fists and deep bruises.

I did not hear them and walked on.

CINDERS

When I got too bored with our town, and driving back country roads with My Only Friend in Town and a joint of Boredom Relief was not an option, I sometimes ran laps at the old high school track. It was a cinder track. Hard-black chucks of coal-slag like gritty black-glass diamonds. I had run on this same track most of my life. Like many folks in town, I had knees permanently scarred and freckled with tiny bits of cinder like rat-shot fired from a starter-gun. We would run this track. Every year of the past, before the new school, our town's kids would congregate there at the old high school track for a grand competition of Youth Games.

High-jump, two-hundred yard dash, one-hundred yard dash, shot-put, discus-throw, baseball-hurl, long-jump, tug-of-war, sweat equaled blue ribbon, red ribbon, white ribbon, yellow ribbon, purple ribbon participation.

Youthful exuberance flowed like a snapshot of childhood determination and will.

I would run on the track sometimes and meditate on adrenaline. The runner's high. Pulling up cinders on the curves and looking smooth on the straight stretches; it made me feel good.

I never wore my earplugs.

I liked to hear the sound of my life on the cinder track. The beating in my chest. The slick crunch of pounding feet into the black slag. My body moving through space like a calorically-generated miracle of panting, puffing, and measured breaths. Almost like I was whole again. Or at least aware in some corporeal state. The return to animal. The path on the Way. The understanding was the doing, and the doing I could hear.

Like the new high school, my problems were Far Away.

At the old high school stadium, the cinder track ringed our town's well-maintained football field. Like Town Lake, the athletic stadium and the high school owed their architectural existence to Big Government and the W.P.A. like the growing pains of world dominance.

After the games, when the only sound that trickled through the muggy summer air was the *spat! spat!* turning of the water sprinklers spitting hell-tainted water onto the green grass and the chalk lines of the football field, My Only Friend in Town and I would venture down beneath the concrete stadium. We would slip in under a rusted-out chain-link fence and enter a dark, damp, and junk-filled world filled with decades of trash like football dandruff. A whole, cool world to explore. A respite from the heat and from the town.

Our own cave.

EARPLUGS

Once, My Only Friend in Town said, "Eww. Hey. Look at this nasty old pair of earplugs I found."

"Gross," I squeaked. "What the hell would you wear those for?"

Above us, the concrete stands hung like ordered M.C. Escher stalactites, cascading down to field level like an upside down stairway. Down where it was so dark we did not dare to go. To get down there you would have to crawl like the resident snakes that left every Friday night of football season to go catch mice, or to shoot some pool, or to do any damn thing but put up with that loud shit.

"God-damned football," the snakes would say, as they slithered on down to crack some mice-balls.

Town High School on the Hill Stadium. Fans poured into the stadium on football Friday nights to cheer for the Black and White, our town's colors, and eat cafeteria pizza from the snack bar like a recaptured vision of their younger selves.

Meanwhile, minions of town hoods would roam the grounds around the cinder track while the preps, the parents, and the populace would pack and gossip in the stands. Hormones filled the air like the foregone conclusion of Odeur Nouveau. The stadium klieg lights shone down on the green grass of night, and on the football warriors, and all about our town. Cheerleaders romped. The band played. Eau de Auld went to bed. Lovers hunkered down to escape the lights behind generations of tombstones in the cemetery below the Winding Trails. Their bodies steamed on the hillside above the stadium. The autumnal smell of burned leaves and of instinctive fellowship electrified the thin frost-laden night air. Downtown, Trainstop slung pizzas and sold gallons of draft beer and pitchers of Pepsi. School fights occurred in abandoned back alleyways like territorial pissing matches. Hunting season began and deer ran about the county wondering what the fuck was going on. The Fair had come and gone; the Derby had rocked and crashed. The town larders were well stocked. With the coming of the frost, our pretty, bountiful hills shed their lovely fall leaves and fell gray into decay and rebirth.

All that was gone now.

The Service Industry and our Town Council, under *Tourism II, Subsection: the Big Box of Education*, had kept up the current national trend of ripping the heart and the school from the community and had moved our town high school out past the edge of town, far to the south. Like the Family Fun for All Center, the new school and the new athletic field sat in an old corn field beside the Meandering River. The new track was polyurethane.

"Town High School on the Floodplain Stadium," said the old veteran farmer, who did not want to pay the taxes.

"YEAHHHHHHHH!" said a high school kid, happy to drive Somewhere Else, which, peculiarly, was now very close.

Parents left town now and drove out to watch their children and to visit their neighbors at the football games like inmates at an educational institution. The klieg lights were still on, but the pizza tasted different, and everyone began to dream their own new dream.

It all stank.

I would run the old black cinder track sometimes when I was too bored, and I would think about good.

And then I would quit, and replace my earplugs.

Bram Riddlebarger writes, plays music, and lives in Athens, Ohio. *Earplugs* is his first novel.